FINDING FAMILY

DIANA DERICCI

Purple Sword Publications
Tucson, AZ

FINDING FAMILY
Copyright © 2015 DIANA DERICCI
ISBN 978-1-61292-146-4
ISBN 10: 1612921469
Cover Art Designed by Anastasia Rabiyah
Edited by Traci Markou

Published by Purple Sword Publications, LLC
Tucson, Arizona, USA
www.PurpleSword.com

The Jasper Series
Reading List:

Tougher to Love
Second Chance Summer
Finding Home
Finding Family

Prologue

Six year-old Chelsea and her twin brother Micah sat as still as they could on the wooden bench. Her brother held his hands clutched together on his lap, and she gripped her slightly worn bear to her thin chest. Fear of the coming moments kept her rigid.

The man behind the high counter was talking to the lawyer, Mr. Jacks, in low, direct tones. She remembered the first time she'd sat right on that bench in front of the man behind the counter, the one dressed in black who barely looked at them, while she'd listened in shivering silence as their lives were changed forever. He hadn't looked happy to see them then, and he didn't look happy now. He kind of scared Chelsea.

Mr. Jacks, he was a nice man. She'd learned he was a lawyer, and that he was there to keep them safe. Whenever he talked to the twins, he spoke in slow, caring tones. She knew he was supposed to be helping them. That was really about all she knew.

"Do you think they'll make us go back to Mama?" Micah whispered at her shoulder. His voice trembled, revealing his deepest fears.

She shook her head vigorously, almost shaking them both off the bench. "Mr. Jacks said we are safe now." She'd clung onto those words like a promise. So far, he'd told the truth. They hadn't seen their mother in a long time. Chelsea missed her because she was familiar, their mother, but she was more glad they weren't going back to her. She hoped.

Micah reached and curled his scrawny fingers over hers. She held his in answer. Sitting a little closer, they huddled together, neither looking away from the two men.

They'd spent the last four months in a home with other kids, some older, a few younger, and one baby. The people who'd been there, Ms. Beverly and Mr. Dawson, had said they were safe, too. That their mama couldn't find them, couldn't hurt them anymore. It terrified her when their mother got angry with them. It was scary going to someone's house to stay, like a sleepover that they never went home from, but the fear of going back to their mother was worse.

"What are they doing?" Micah asked.

"Just talking." Chelsea had no better idea than he did, and she hadn't looked away once.

"Thank you, Judge Barton." Mr. Jacks closed his case and turned to the kids. He smiled. Chelsea's heart pounded. Something huge was about to change. All he'd said when he'd picked them up that morning was he had to take them to talk to the judge. She didn't know if they were going back to the home with all of the kids or not.

After walking up to them, he knelt in front of them on a single knee. "I have good news for the both of you," he said with the calm assurance that Chelsea recognized.

Neither of the children made a peep at his declaration though.

"Now, I know it's been scary—"

"Please don't make us go back to Mama!" Micah blurted. Chelsea held his hand tighter, squeezing to hold him closer. He trembled beside her, fear coursing through them both.

Mr. Jacks startled, his eyes shooting wide at Micah's outburst. "Shh. I know it's going to be hard but you're safe, the both of you. Your mother can never hurt you again. As of today, she'll never know where you are, either."

Chelsea tipped her head. "Never?"

He spoke to Micah, then Chelsea, including both. "Never. Right now, we're going to make sure you and Chelsea are safe, with warm beds and kind people who will care for you."

"Like Ms. Beverly?" Chelsea asked.

"A lot like Ms. Beverly," he replied. "We need to take a road trip, an adventure. There's a very nice couple who want to meet you."

"Can Mr. Bear come?"

Mr. Jacks smiled softly. "I'd never leave him behind. Yes, he can come." He stood, slipping the strap of his case over a shoulder, and offered a hand to each of the children.

They slid to their feet, unsure, sharing glances.

"Why don't we stop for food? I bet you two are hungry."

Micah nodded his head, though he didn't look up.

"Can I have fries?" Chelsea asked.

Mr. Jacks carefully guided his charges from the courtroom. "I bet I can find a place that has fries." He jiggled Micah's hand. "What do you say, Micah? French fries sound good?"

"Yes, please," he said.

Chelsea heard the hesitant hitch in Micah's answer, terrified he'd be hit, or worse, for whatever he'd done wrong. She looked up at Mr. Jacks and only found a smile. No anger. What she saw helped her breathe a little easier as they left the building. Everything was going to be all right. Mr. Jacks said so.

They followed Mr. Jacks to his car. It always made her stare when he could press a button and the van sides just rolled backward. He called it his modern day spaceship. Once they were both buckled up in their seats and he made sure they were secure, the doors glided shut to lock.

He climbed in and started the engine. "I know it's scary, not knowing what's going to happen. Just know that where you're going, they want you. The both of you."

Micah twisted on his booster and watched through the tinted window as the van started to move. Because of space between the seats, Chelsea couldn't reach for him. She didn't say it, but she was just as scared.

She clutched Mr. Bear a little tighter.

Chapter One

Four months earlier

Parker steadied Summer on the pony's saddle. "Good?" he asked before letting her go. She nodded briskly, her little hands tight on the horn. He handed her the reins and adjusted her grip. "You remember the last session, right? The rules?"

"I do." Her cheeks were flushed with excitement, and the breezy cold of a clinging winter being reborn into spring. Still cold enough for a coat, that was for sure. He checked the stirrups for her again then stepped clear.

"Good. Okay, make Sugar walk."

She tapped her heels and the small horse began to make the circle around the pen.

"Good. You're doing good." His cell phone buzzed at his hip. "Vandersoot Training," he said to answer it.

"That sounds so nice."

Parker smiled. "Hello, handsome." He kept a sharp eye on the girl riding the pony, spinning on a boot heel as they made the round. "Aren't you supposed to be at a conference?"

"I am, just had to call and hear your voice. I miss you."

"Miss you too," he replied, not even trying to hide the longing he felt. It had been a lonely week with Will in New York.

"I'll be home in two days. Two days too long for me."

Parker harrumphed at Will's complaining. "Just get through them and get home."

"I will. New York is freezing. I'll need all kinds of activity to warm back up."

That made Parker chuckle.

"I need to get back. This break is almost over. Love you."

"Love you too," Parker offered, feeling warmer hearing his man's voice. They said their goodbyes and Parker walked up to Sugar's side. Summer eased the pony to a stop. "Keep your legs about here, not pulled up." She nodded and readjusted on the saddle. "I know it's stretching your legs but you'll get used to it." He gave Sugar a good cheek scratch then moved away. "Okay, make him go again. Remember, he only does what you tell him. He'll stand there and fall asleep if you don't tell him what you want."

He worked with Summer for another half hour then called her done. "You did good today."

She smiled up at him. Parker made sure she helped unsaddle then brush down Sugar. "Good job. Go grab a carrot from the box."

She leaped out of the stall and came clomping back with a carrot chunk. "Thank you, Sugar." He took his treat, huffing a sigh that Parker recognized as *I'm done* in horse speak.

"Let's let him out for the afternoon." He handed her the rope, staying right at Sugar's head as she guided him to the open door. The latch was unclipped from the halter and Parker gave him a push to go. He went out about five feet into the sunshine, stopped, and lowered his head. *I hear ya. Totally done.* Grazing was minimal but it was the outside more than the grass he gave the horses every day. Being cooped up did them no good.

"Let's finish cleaning up. Your Mimi will be here soon to pick you up."

Parker wasn't wrong. Ten minutes later, Jeannie, one of Summer's moms, rolled their SUV behind the house to the barn. Jeannie waved and after a hug from Summer for Parker, she trotted over and clambered into her seat. He stopped at the open driver side window to talk.

"She behave herself?" Jeannie asked

"Always does," he replied.

Jeannie just smiled. "I do not know what magic you have, but I'm glad you have it with her."

Parker just chuckled. He knew Summer behaved around him because she wanted to. Given half a chance, she'd be like any typical four year-old.

"Bye Parker! Thank you!" Summer called from the back seat.

"Bye, baby girl. I'll see you on Sunday."

He stepped away from the vehicle and let them leave, returning to the barn with a wandering pace. With Summer's lesson over, he had a few hours to kill before he had to bring in the horses for the night.

He got to work on the stall cleaning, changing hay and filling water. To some, it probably looked like what it was— plain, hard work, but he loved it. He loved being with the horses, loved working with them.

As he finished the stalls, he lingered by one in particular. He ran a thumb over the plaque screwed to the gate. *Tank*. His baby. A gift from his man. He'd had a horse before, but his father had sold him at some point after his father had kicked him off their ranch in Texas. A lot had changed in his life since he'd found his own place again, there in Jasper.

He'd gone from a homeless nobody without family, to a loved man with more family than could fill a house, a caring man to call his own, even a sister thanks to Summer. Her big brother nickname had stuck. She'd be starting kindergarten that fall. The school system didn't have a clue of what they were getting in her. He chuckled, then resumed his cleaning and fussing.

He tended to stay in the barn extra late when Will wasn't home, and tonight wasn't an exception. He'd moved in right after Valentine's Day, finally conceding to Will's wishes and judgment, that he needed to be there. It wasn't an easy decision.

The couple he'd been boarding with, Ian and Caleb, had saved his hide, in more ways than there were blades of grass. He owed them, probably more than he'd ever be able to pay back in this lifetime.

Homeless for nearly four years after his father had disowned him for being gay, he'd all but stumbled into Jasper, a hitchhiker with little to his name. Ian had fed him, clothed him, even gave him a job. And slowly, Parker began to heal from the inside out.

Will was another good thing that had happened in Jasper. Well, meeting him, not the reason why he'd needed to see a dentist. His jaw where the damaged tooth had been had healed and thanks to Will's care, he wouldn't be losing any more of his teeth. Parker almost chuckled. Now he grew impatient to see his dentist, instead of avoiding them.

Parker taught riding lessons and cared for the barn's upkeep and management. It was his type of work to the core. Earth, horse, and sun. Well, when it wasn't freezing outside. That was one thing they didn't *quite* have on the Texas gulf coast— snowy winters. He turned back to his work with a lighter step.

He was putting away tools when his cell phone buzzed again. "Vandersoot Training."

"Hey, man."

"Travis." Parker smiled, happy to hear from his friend. "How'd you do?"

"Second behind Cody Wilhelm in the standings."

"That's amazing!" Parker cheered.

"A hell of a lot better than I thought I'd do this year, considering. Still a long way to go."

"And Eddie?"

"Fifth. He had a bad round last weekend."

"Damn."

Travis' sigh was heavy over the phone. "Yeah."

"So can you guys swing through?"

"I have to head home for a week or so, but I think we can drive out next month. We're taking a break for now."

"Awesome! Bring your horses. We'll go riding."

"You bet."

And Will would be home. It would be great to see Travis and Eddie again. It wasn't the first time they'd stayed over since Parker had reconnected with his best friend. Travis had been a best friend, a brother, and a first crush. He cherished the friendship that had survived after all they'd both been through, and their visit gave him something to look forward to.

Friday, he drove to Des Moines to pick up Will at the airport. Stopping in the loading alley, he turned on the hazard lights and hopped out of the car, the slap of his boots muffled with all the other noise. Cars, voices, the roar of airplanes. It was a wonder people could think at all with the cacophony surrounding them.

Will had seen him and was scurrying over, toting his bags while juggling his coat and a carry-on bag. "God, I'm glad to be home," he uttered.

Parker cupped his cheek, stroking lightly at his face. Shadows lay deep under his man's eyes. "It looks like it. They did let you sleep, right?"

"As much as I could. Just so much going on. Lectures, technique discussion, new laws. My head is still spinning."

Parker gave him a soft, greeting kiss. "Then let's load up and get you home." After tossing luggage and suit bags into the trunk, they started home. Parker didn't say one word when Will fell asleep on the drive to Jasper.

"We're home." He shook Will's leg lightly once they were in front of the house.

Will moaned, stretching. "I'm sorry."

"You needed it. You're home now. That's the important thing to me."

"Did Isis miss me?"

"I think she did. She kept nosing at me when I brushed down Tank. She missed the company."

That made Will smile. "I missed our rides. It's getting warm again."

Parker knew what that meant. Will loved riding in the evenings after he closed his dental office for the day. It was their time.

First things first, a hot shower, and then he'd pour his man into bed to let him feel home.

* * * *

The next morning, Parker was whipping up breakfast, trying to get it all together before Will woke up. Centering the plate on the tray, he poured coffee into Will's favorite mug, making it the way he liked, and with it on the corner, carefully lifted the tray. With cautious steps, he traversed from the kitchen to the bedroom, pushing the slightly ajar door open with an elbow.

Will blinked his eyes open when Parker cleared his throat. He didn't want to just wake him up, but if he happened to wake up, then...

"Morning," Parker said warmly in greeting, beaming at the rumpled handsomeness in the bed.

"Morning," Will answered. "What's that?" He ran a hand over his face, propping up on an elbow to study Parker.

"A welcome home present."

Will smiled. "You didn't have to."

Parker rolled a shoulder, mindful of his hands. "Wanted to."

Will sat up in bed, fluffing pillows to lean against. He patted the blankets and Parker rested the tray over Will's legs.

"This looks good."

Parker flushed a little at the praise. He knew his cooking left a lot to be desired. "I'm still trying." He sat at the opposite end of the bed by Will's feet to not disturb him. He wasn't surprised either when the first thing he went for was the coffee. Will moaned in appreciation.

"I think I missed that the most. Just a regular cup of coffee." He returned the mug and gazed at a silent Parker. "What's wrong, cowboy?"

He curled up on the bed, crossing his legs, lightly stroking the top of Will's foot hidden beneath the blankets. He wasn't exactly avoiding Will, but he couldn't seem to look up, either. "I don't know how to ask," he finally admitted.

"Usually with words is a good place to start," Will teased.

Parker grumbled under his breath, more laughter than annoyance. After a pause, he started with, "You know I love you, and I've never felt more for anyone else."

"Parker." Will shifted the tray to the nightstand and reached toward him. "This isn't like you. What's wrong?"

Parker crawled forward and rested against Will's chest. "What do you think of kids?" He curled into his man's body. He'd missed him like crazy the whole week he was gone. Holding him was heaven.

"The furry, four-legged type, or the type that require school grades?"

Parker smiled, snuffling into the blankets as he held on a little tighter. "School grade kind."

Will didn't react, or answer, right away. Parker almost held his breath. He'd been wanting to ask since Christmas, but everything in its own time. That was something he'd learned from Will.

He honestly felt now was the time. He and Will were going strong, the training was starting to pick up, and Will had fully integrated into Jasper by taking over the old dentist's practice. Neither one of them were going anywhere.

"Are you ready for kids? You're still young yourself," Will mentioned.

Parker rocked against the arms holding him. "I know." He was twenty-one, which in the common world was an adult, but by most was still too young for what he was wanting. A family. "And I also know that's going to go against us." He dared to arch on his neck to stare into Will's beautiful eyes. "I want to try. Adoptions are legal for us. Maybe even foster."

"But we're not married," Will stated.

Parker stiffened and tried to move away. Will refused to let him, keeping him close.

"I'm not saying no," he told Parker. "I am saying, is now the right time?"

Parker snuggled into Will again. "I've thought about this for months, not a few days."

Will fell silent for several minutes. Then he surprised Parker by asking, "Why children?"

Parker could answer that easily, and truthfully. "Because I want to give someone the home I didn't have. A loving home."

"Aww, cowboy." Will tugged him even closer until Parker was resting his forehead to Will's jaw.

Parker wanted them both to do it, to want it, but he wasn't going to push Will into a corner. He hadn't really thought about the married aspect. To him, they were together, they were living together, in the same bed, sharing the same house and responsibilities. But...Will was right. That was also going to cause them problems.

"I guess you're right." He sighed. "It's only since I've been here, really since I've known Summer, that I wanted to have what Jeannie and Wanda have."

"A little girl of your own?" Will guessed.

"Or a boy," he replied, more than a little wistfully. "Dad was a selfish, abusive bastard. Ian and Caleb changed my life. Then you changed me." He blinked because he still got emotional when it snuck up on him. Too much of it was still fresh in his memory. It hadn't been a full year since Ian had all but saved Parker on that Jasper sidewalk, more than likely from a slow death with all he'd been through. Underweight, underfed, and a serious infection that was just waiting to happen. He swallowed to get the rush of emotions under control. Will was the only one he allowed to see him like this.

Will urged Parker's chin upward, gazing into his eyes, searching. "You've always been more than your age. It just took me time to see that. I believe you when you say you've thought about this. But..." Will swept a thumb over Parker's jaw. "I think it would look a lot better on any paperwork if we're already married."

Parker nodded, hiding his disappointment. He'd figured there would be some reason. Maybe Will would want to in a year or two. "I know." It was a lot to spring on him anyway, since the topic had never been brought up between them. At least he wasn't against kids entirely.

Will ran fingers through loose strands on Parker's head, lulling him with the easy caresses as they cuddled. Parker knew his hair was one of Will's weak spots.

"Will you marry me?" Will asked quietly a few minutes later.

Parker didn't know how to react. He arched his frame, pushing up on the bed. "Are you serious?" He certainly hadn't expected it.

"Well, if you're serious about wanting to start a family, we're both going into it, right?"

Parker's eyes slowly widened as what he was hearing finally clicked. He swallowed. Hard. "You want to marry me?"

"I love you, cowboy. A family isn't something I'll do lightly. It will change everything."

That sounded ominous. "Will it change us?"

Will gave him a patient smile. "Yes and no. It will never change what I feel for you, but if we start a family, then we're no longer just *us*." He studied Parker closely. "Are you ready for that?"

Was he? He felt like he was. Parker also knew no matter what they did, they wouldn't be starting their family that day, or the next.

"Everything in its own time," he said and Will's lips curled upward.

"Is that a yes? That was an honest proposal."

Parker reached upward and kissed him tenderly. "Yes."

What surprised him even more, because it was so unexpected, was the relief and happiness glowing in Will's eyes. Parker's answer had really mattered.

"Love you," Will whispered as their lips touched.

Parker's feelings weren't hurt that he had to cook breakfast twice that morning.

Chapter Two

At the weekly Sunday breakfast with Ian, Caleb, and the rest of the family, the news of Parker's and Will's plans were loudly, happily, received. Parker would have been surprised if it hadn't been. Boisterous was something this family did well.

Brice hugged him, overjoyed. "So happy for the both of you!"

Caleb shook Will's hand. "Welcome to the family."

"I guess this does make it official, huh?" Will joked.

Since Parker had moved in with Will, he'd become a permanent part of the family and all their mish-mash gatherings. Parker was sure everyone had assumed it was only a matter of time for this announcement to happen.

"When do you think you'll do it?" Vivian asked.

Parker drank some water to clear his throat as chatter eased a bit around the table for everyone to listen. "Well, actually, Travis and Eddie are coming up next month to visit. They're breaking between sessions."

"Want to do it then? When they're here?" Will suggested.

"That would be awesome." Having his friends there along with his adopted family would be the icing to this cake.

"We can plan a wedding in a month," Vivian said, rubbing her round stomach. She was glowing with her pregnancy. "Do you want to invite anyone else?"

Parker looked to Caleb. "Would the rest of your family want to be here?" He wouldn't deny the two men who'd done so much for him, or their family.

"It has been a while since Jessie dragged everyone down," he mused. He and Ian shared a quiet glance. "Yeah, let's do that. A wedding party."

"Are you okay with that?" Parker asked Will.

"Works for me. Mom and Dad will fly out, too."

"Is there room for everyone?" Parker wondered. There was Jessie and his bunch, Aaron and Terra, and Becky, whom he hadn't met yet. Then Will's parents. That was a lot of extra people.

"We'll make room," Brice was quick to offer.

"Well, hot damn," Wanda said, smiling brightly. "We have a wedding to plan!"

Parker reached for Will's hand under the table and gripped it, both smiling broadly at the cheering and rush of talk escalating around the table now.

"You know, you just handed them *carte blanche* to go crazy," Will said.

"Yeah. Isn't it great?"

Will laughed at his side, pressing his forehead into Parker's shoulder to hide the worst of it.

* * * *

The following three weeks flew by as their wedding neared.

"It's good to shift gears and just ride," Travis was saying at Parker's side. He patted Snowman on the neck. The creak of leather saddles and the occasional twitch of heads jangled bridles. The easy plod of their horses' gaits was exactly what they'd all needed. "Been a while since we've done this."

"It has," Parker agreed. Details for his and Will's ceremony, and his friends' pending visit, had filled his head and his days. A lot of things to look forward to. Travis and Eddie had driven in the night before and now they were all enjoying an afternoon ride. He glanced over his shoulder, checking on Will and Eddie. They had chummed up like two best pals. Seeing his man happy always made Parker a little giddy. "I'm glad you could be here for the ceremony."

Travis' head rocked. "Could've knocked me over with a feather when you told us that." But by the gleam in his gaze, Parker knew he was happy for them.

"Have you and Eddie – "

Travis was quick to frown. "No. He hasn't even moved in yet. I'm trying."

Parker hadn't expected that. He tipped up the brim of his hat with a finger to stare at his friend. "Why not? I thought he would have been ready to after the holidays." Eddie and his sister had stayed with Travis over Thanksgiving and that had looked extremely cozy to him. Not moving in made zilch sense to Parker.

Travis sighed roughly. "He's still antsy about it. Being at home isn't the same as when we're on the road."

"At home?" Almost as soon as Parker said it, he knew. "Kyle." He managed to not growl the name. Just.

"He's a real bastard. A damned lot like your father."

Parker absently wound reins over his hands, thinking. "It's none of his business." It did make him curious about what kind of shit Kyle was causing them. If he was bad-mouthing his friends, or causing problems with other land owners. Why, Parker had no idea, but the man was bitter, and clearly vindictive.

His hate made no sense though. The man had gotten everything when Parker's father had died. Parker's old man had deeded the entire ranch and all its assets to his last foreman, writing Parker completely out of his will after he'd kicked him out of his life years before. What could he possibly have to bitch about?

"It's not just him. Eddie is out to his family. Hell. The man is twenty-six. Doesn't mean they're fully supportive."

"That sucks," Parker sympathized.

"They're not crazy about me, either."

That shocked Parker. "Why the hell not!"

Travis hiked a shoulder, but Parker could see it bothered him. "White boy. Non-Catholic, and I don't want to be."

"Wow," Parker gasped. "Is he pushing at you to change?"

"Nope. And I'm grateful, but if I don't, they'll never approve, and..." He took a deep breath. "He'll never do what you and Will are doing without it."

"I doubt that," Parker argued. He knew Eddie cared too damned much to let prejudices stop him.

By the forlorn look in Travis' eyes, he wasn't as convinced.

"Have you asked him?"

Travis harrumphed. "He won't even move in." He scratched absently at a horse shoulder. "I love him. I know I do. I know he loves me. He's the man I want. But..."

"He's not making it easy for you."

"No, he's not."

"Bastard," Parker joked.

Travis laughed roughly.

Parker nudged Tank a little closer so he could lower his voice. "What if you...you know. Here. With us?"

"Move in?"

Parker slapped his side for being dense. "No. Ceremony," he whispered.

"Oh... Oh!" Travis stopped Snowman with a light pull on the reins. "Are you serious?"

"Let me make sure Will doesn't mind sharing the day," he said. "If he says it's okay, then it's up to you."

Travis looked a little wild for a few seconds, his eyes wide. Parker got them both moving again before Eddie and Will caught up too close. They were far enough behind that anything less than a raised voice wouldn't reach them, but he didn't want to take any chances.

"Let him know you're serious. It just might be the shock he needs."

"His family – "

"Do you want to marry his family? Or him?" Parker asked solemnly. Without a lick of warning, he spun Tank to join Will at his side. "Hey Eddie, quit hogging my man." Taking his cue from Parker, Travis did the same on the other side, riding four abreast on the roadside.

"Did you know Eddie is only four credits shy of a psyche major?" Will said as soon as he'd settled Tank to walk next to Will's Isis.

Parker shook his head. "That's awesome. I'm working on a business management degree myself."

"Is that to help with the training?" Eddie asked.

"A lot, yeah. Plus running the barn as a service. A lot of paperwork." He groaned. Will gave him a humored grin.

"So, are you two really going through with this next weekend?"

Parker shared a tender, knowing look with Will, then answered Eddie. "It's only the first step. We want to adopt."

Travis did a low whistle. "Wow. You sure?"

"Not happening tomorrow," Will and Parker said at the same time. They laughed deeply at the shared sentiment. They'd talked a lot about it, and their future since they'd decided to put things into motion. Parker hadn't ever been happier, and he knew Will felt the same with a mission and a goal in view.

"We've written up the first plan of intent and once we can add married and stable to the application, we'll be sending it in." Will reached for one of Parker's hands, squeezing. "I'm actually starting to look forward to it."

"So...kids, huh?" Travis adjusted his hat and glanced toward Parker.

Parker said, "After my dad, what he did, I know I can do better. I know there are kids out there in need."

"Besides, after talking to the agency, we're looking at months minimum, to find where and how we can help. We're open to fostering, also," Will added.

"You're both good role models. Hard working, caring." Travis patted the horse beneath him. "All I've ever had was the furry kind of kids, and they're a handful of their own."

"Do you want kids?" Eddie asked.

Travis shrugged. "Someday. Maybe. I don't know."

Parker noticed Eddie was hanging on Travis' every word, while he was shying away from actually giving an answer.

When he sat forward, Eddie rolled his shoulders and heaved a short breath, finally giving Parker and Will a tight smile that eventually relaxed.

"I know you two will be great dads. I saw you with that little one last summer. You'll do fine."

"Thanks Eddie." Will touched Parker's thigh. "Ready to head back? I'm getting hungry."

"Sure."

"Is Parker cooking?" Travis asked with teasing laughter. "'Cause my insurance hasn't been paid this month."

"Butthead," Parker growled.

"He's not that bad," Will said in his defense.

That mollified him a little. "Thank you."

"But close," Will tacked on, ducking a playful jab from Parker right after. "Love you, cowboy."

Rough grumbling made them all laugh.

* * * *

"So, what do you think?" Parker asked Will that night as they were getting ready for bed.

"They won't have time to do a license, but they could do a commitment ceremony," Will offered thoughtfully. He turned to Parker who was nearing from the bathroom. He couldn't believe how his cowboy turned him on, yet just knowing they were together made him the happiest he'd ever been. Walking in wearing only pajama bottoms showed off his flat abs and smooth chest. He'd regained a lot of the muscle and healthy weight he'd lost in the years he'd been wandering the roads after his father had disowned him days before his seventeenth birthday. The man he was becoming before Will's eyes made him feel like he was the luckiest in the world to have Parker's affections. Loyal, caring, hard-working. Parker may be young, but he was mature beyond his years, honed by hard times that were forced on him. Will was glad he'd finally seen his maturity before he'd come close to losing Parker because he'd been unsure about the nearly ten year age difference.

Will reached a hand and Parker took it, curling fingers together to be pulled to the bed. "I doubt the JP would say no. It'll take, what? Maybe an extra fifteen minutes?"

"I'm not sure Travis will do it, but there's something going on there. A little push might be what it takes to make them both come around."

"Yeah, I saw it too, about the kids." Will slid under the blankets, bringing Parker with him. "They need to talk." Will tucked them in, ensuring Parker's behind was covered. He had a tendency to wiggle out from under the covers in the middle of the night.

"But if Eddie won't meet him in the middle to be a couple..." Parker sighed. "I hate seeing Travis hurt like that. He's my best friend, after you."

Will smiled, burying it in Parker's hair. He knew where he stood with Parker. "They'll come around. Just like we did."

"Love you," Parker murmured drowsily against Will's chest.

"Love my cowboy," Will echoed. He nuzzled with his chin into Parker's hair, feeling the younger man drift into sleep. He didn't mind sharing their wedding day with Travis and Eddie. It would be kind of fun, actually. Will did like the two of them, though he'd been nervous when Parker had to unexpectedly return to Texas last November when he'd learned his father had passed away.

Travis had been Parker's first kiss. His best friend growing up, riding horses and competing together as junior bull riders. However, the strength of the welcome kiss Will had received when he'd shown up unannounced at the Texas ranch for Parker's father's funeral had destroyed unshakable fears digging into his conscience. A deep friendship was what had survived between the two, rather than surviving affections or longing for each other.

Will couldn't help holding him a little closer knowing that Parker loved him. He was one tough guy having lived through years of hardship to come out resilient and deeply thoughtful on the other side.

That calmness was one of the reasons Will believed Parker's desires to have children were sound. He had youth and energy, and hard-earned wisdom. Will had his parents, whom he could rely on, and age. Plus they both had all of Parker's adoptive family there in Jasper, and there was nothing this family wouldn't do if a person needed a hand up.

Heck, their wedding was being planned by his soon to be sister-in-laws, and from what they'd shared, it was going to be elegant, but scaled to suit the smaller gathering of family and friends. Parker and he had both offered suggestions and the girls had promised to give them as much of what they wanted as they could. It would be part of their gift to them. Well, the planning part of it because both he and Parker had admitted quickly that wasn't something either knew one thing about. The girls were doing exceptionally well to stay in budget, too, which Will wouldn't deny made him happy.

"And then you'll be my husband," he whispered to not disturb a sleeping Parker. The one thing he'd never been sure he'd find. He hadn't been actively hunting to find a man to connect with, though he had met several men before moving to Iowa. More than a new life and job had waited for him when he got there.

Hearing Parker mumble at his continued restlessness Will relaxed, attempting sleep for himself. He needed his rest for the morning anyway. Sunday breakfast was always an adventure, and Travis and Eddie were going to be lucky enough to be subjected to their brand of crazy. At least this wasn't their weekend to host.

He was smiling when sleep finally claimed him, happy in ways he could never put into words.

Chapter Three

Parker futzed with his tie, staring at it in the mirror the following Saturday afternoon. The closest he'd ever gotten to a tie was a bolo. He didn't even know how to fix the stupid thing so it looked straight. Jeannie did it for him. He'd been staring at his reflection trying to find himself in the clothing for the last twenty minutes. Between the pressed slacks, overcoat, tie and whatever that was – the flower pinned to the jacket – it was a lost cause. He knew it was a rose, but that was all he knew. He couldn't for the life of him remember what they were called.

Jeannie shook her head and slapped his hands away from the tie and anything else he could mangle. "Quit. You look incredible."

Parker flushed. "I've never worn a tux. Was this necessary?" He tugged on the fabric at his waist. "What the hell is this thing, anyway?"

"It's called a cummerbund. And yes, it's very traditional for men to wear tuxes to weddings, especially their own." She *tsked* when she caught his rising hand again. "It's too warm to do the double-breasted variety. You'll survive the few hours you're not in denim. I promise you."

Parker just blinked at her via his reflection. He didn't know what double-breasted was, or why it mattered. He wasn't about to ask and look more stupid, either.

He drew a breath. He supposed he didn't look too bad. The suit – tux – was a dull black, with a lighter charcoal tie and waist thing – cummerbund – he quickly corrected himself. It was just so foreign. Definitely not jeans and boots. And no hat. He missed his hat something fierce. He wore some sort of fancy shoes too. *So not me.* But he'd happily wear it all for Will. His love had been quietly excited about being in something besides work scrubs or jeans at home. He got the feeling Will liked getting all duded up. *For him, anything,* he mentally whispered.

"Besides," she told him, breaking into his musings. "In a few years, you're going to want to have proof to show you did this."

"Don't you mean memories?"

She smiled broadly with full blown humor. "Yeah, those too."

He groaned. Jeannie gave him a kind squeezed hug around the waist. She turned to look in the mirror with him, standing below his shoulder. "You really are a looker. Will is a lucky man."

Parker swallowed, his throat growing a little tight. "You think so? Lucky?" He pushed loose hair away from his face. Now that the moment was here, he'd been drowning in waves of nerves all day.

"Without a doubt. And I know he feels the same way."

There was a quick tapping on the door, then Ian popped his head into the room. "You two ready? Will and Wanda are."

Parker stiffened his shoulders, willing his heart to calm. It helped, but only a little. "As ready as I'll ever be." Ian smiled in understanding and backed out of the room.

Jeannie offered an arm. "Let's get you hitched, handsome."

Parker barked a nervous laugh and curled Jeannie's hand over an arm to be escorted to the front of the hall.

Will had mentioned a church wedding but Parker had mostly nixed it. He wasn't of any religion and didn't see the point in adding an extra cost when a hall would be just as good – one stop and done. The JP had also been warmly welcoming to their marriage. Parker had dreaded trying to find a preacher who'd be unbiased. It was the lack of prejudice that had immensely comforted Parker. There was no doubt that his father's actions had deeply scarred him, bringing fears rising to the surface as they'd come to agreements on the details.

The girls had decorated the hall with some help from the family, with large bows on the walls, and a couple of white and yellow flower arrangements on side tables. It was actually very simple. There was another table loaded with food, and a huge cake that he couldn't wait to dive into waited in a corner. He knew perfectly well that was Wanda and Jeannie's personal gift to them. Parker had liked everything on sight when he'd first arrived that afternoon to change from Parker, the working ranch hand, to Parker, the groom-to-be.

He released a pent-up breath as they neared the opened doors that would let them into the main hall. Basically, both were being escorted to the aisle, where they'd join hands and walk the distance to the JP together. A symbolic statement that from this moment forward, every step they took would be as one.

Standing at the base of the aisle, he saw a few faces beginning to swing in his direction. Travis, Eddie, Ian, Caleb. Family and friends. His family.

He blinked and swallowed. His emotions were a wreck today. He wrestled to get them under control.

The soft sound of steps and the swish of fabric yanked him to look to his left.

"Damn," he breathed in hushed awe. He'd never seen Will look so...hot. The tux definitely added something very sophisticated to the man.

Will blushed, tipping his chin a slight hair as he returned the stare and the smile. "Hey, cowboy."

Wanda released Will to Parker's care to find Jeannie's hand. "Don't forget you two have someplace to be," she teased. She clasped Jeannie's fingers and they walked up the aisle to sit on the front row with Summer between them.

"Ready to do this?" Will asked.

"Oh, hell." He gulped then trembled. His heart tried to leap through his chest in an unstoppable flood of nerves.

"Parker?" Will asked, suddenly concerned.

"So fucking glad I have you." If Will had been anyone else, Parker was sure he'd have high-tailed it out of there like his ass was on fire. *Must be love.* The humor in the Beatles refrain coursing through the thought – where it came from, he had no idea – helped the tension ease from his shoulders.

Will relaxed in a rush. "Then let's make it legal." He offered a hand for Parker to hold. Luckily, Will didn't complain when it was with a death grip when he did.

He honestly didn't remember taking that walk, or finally coming to a stop before the man who was going to do the deed.

Parker's mind had officially become mush. He was standing in front of the sexiest man he'd ever known, quietly taking the vows that would make Will his until the end of forever.

They exchanged rings, the smooth metal odd yet comforting at the same time as it finally came to rest on his finger. Will had chosen them, and Parker loved it. A narrow, single band with small embedded diamonds. It was smooth to the touch to not snag as he went about his workday.

He raised his chin and locked gazes with his man. His husband.

When the kiss came he almost melted to the floor. If he'd ever had any doubt – what sane man wouldn't! – they were slain and laid to rest by that kiss. Will's hand cupped his cheek, a gentle caress that went bone deep, and then heart deep.

"Love you so much," Will murmured against his lips.

Parker swallowed, hunting for his voice. When he couldn't find it, he framed Will's face in trembling palms and kissed him again, telling him without words what that moment, what he, meant to him.

It was several heartbeats, if not longer, before the raucous applause and cheering finally broke into his cotton-wrapped brain. Will's lashes fluttered as he seemed to come out of the ether also.

"Wow," Will murmured. Then he smiled, a caring, shared smile that Parker would always remember.

Will twined their fingers together. Somehow, he seemed to remember to face the crowd on their feet cheering for them and raised Parker's hand in triumph. The volume shook the walls.

* * * *

"That was some kiss," Travis teased. "I was praying they had fire extinguishers."

"Ha ha," Parker retorted. He knew his face was bright red, though. He felt the heat. He'd completely blanked out on the roomful of people there to witness everything. He wanted to relive that kiss until his last day. Because he couldn't help himself, he hunted faces until he found Will, who was standing to the side with his parents, laughing in the lull as things were moved around for the after-party. Now that the legal part was done, it was time to have fun with family and friends.

"So, you know the JP will be here for a bit," Parker hinted, facing Travis again.

Travis' lips quirked. Parker knew he wasn't considering it. Not yet.

"What? Just grab him without warning?" He scoffed.

"It would be fun to watch." Parker chuckled. "Okay, maybe more than fun," he conceded.

Travis snickered.

Parker took a drink from his cup. The champagne was already flowing as people mingled. Summer had given her approval of the punch, the unleaded one. It was green, which she thought was magic.

"Where is he?" Parker asked innocently.

Travis looked over a shoulder, spotting the man in question talking to Brice. His head swiveled the other way, finally stopping when he spotted the Justice of the Peace talking to Jeannie and Wanda. Parker waited for the chain to snap as he looked at both twice more, for the brain to make the do-or-die connection. The man's heart was on his sleeve as much as his thoughts were on his face.

"You know what? You're right. If he truthfully won't marry me because of his family, he better understand I'm not letting him go. He's going to have to make the choice." He handed Parker his mostly empty cup and stalked away to speak to the JP, clearly in fight mode, to get the man of his dreams...*now*. Not two minutes later, he walked over to Eddie, making apologies for stealing him away.

Almost dragging the other man, they halted in front of the JP. Eddie sputtered as the truth was laid out for him.

"You're serious?"

"As a heart attack. Now. Here." Travis was slowly becoming bullish over the decision. Eddie was trapped.

Parker inched closer. He hid crossed fingers behind his back. *Please don't hurt him, Eddie.*

"But...Parker...Will," Eddie choked out.

"Are fine with it," Parker supplied, removing his one chance of meaningful escape.

"Eddie. I've asked. Today, right now, show me you mean it."

Eddie blanched, if that's what it could be called given his skin tone. "But...there's so much..." he hedged.

"We'll work it out." Travis clasped Eddie's hands in his. "That's what this means. We, together."

Parker felt Will's touch on his spine then an arm around his waist. Several more had formed a loose circle around them.

Eddie swept the crowd with a bright gaze that revealed his fear, anxiousness, and underneath everything else, his want. Parker knew the man cared. Sometimes it takes an ultimatum, or a grand-assed shove, to get the point across.

"You have our blessing, Eddie. Make today special," Will told them. Parker leaned into Will's side, relishing the closeness.

Eddie gulped a dry, harsh sound that probably echoed through the hall. He faced Travis then the man patiently waiting beside them. "I – What does it mean?" he managed, hoarsely.

"Only what you want to make of it," the JP explained. He stood with his hands relaxed in his pockets. Sharing in the festivities. No pressure. "This isn't bound by legal agreement, but by your hearts, by intentions. The filed paper is a formality if you both truly believe in what you want to share, here, today."

Eddie seemed to digest that in silence.

"I know how your family feels about me. If you can't do this here and now because of them, then you'll never marry me, anywhere, regardless of what we are to each other." Travis seemed to be losing heart the longer Eddie remained unmoved. His shoulders began to sink while his hands lowered in increments where he held onto Eddie. "I'm fighting for you." As the silence lengthened, a sorrow-filled heaviness grew between them. Travis sighed, his chin sagging last. "I love you, but I guess it's really not enough."

He went to let Eddie's hands slip away, but Parker saw when Eddie caught him firmly, refusing to let go.

"There will be things we will talk about," he stated. It was Eddie's turn to make the rules.

Travis blinked, nodding without argument.

Eddie turned to the JP. "I give my heart to this man because he's already, long before now, given me his." He faced Travis. He let out a slow breath, a life-changing decision finally faced. And made. "My family will either learn to love you like I do, or they will lose. I choose you." Eddie finally smiled and Parker swore the sun rose for Travis.

The JP nodded happily. "Shall we gather in friendship to witness the committed joining of these two men?"

Ten minutes later, another round of applause filled the hall, this time for Parker's best friend and his partner as they shared their first kiss as a joined couple in the eyes of their friends.

Chapter Four

Melody tamped the pages in her hands together on her desk. She'd just signed the final approval to forward their application and the agency recommendation to the state human services to put Will and Parker on the consideration rolls for fostering.

"So that's it?" Parker asked. That couldn't be it. Was it?

Parker felt adrift. And hollow. Like something wasn't finished. After more than two months of interviews, classes, home visits, phone calls, and letters, they were done. Only they weren't. The news was harder to take than he thought it would be.

"That's it. For now. The initial interviews are usually the hardest, but you two came through them all with flying colors."

Will and Parker sat side by side in matching chairs at the adoption agency office in Des Moines. Pictures of happy children of all ages, races, and ethnicities plastered one wall, some with small stickers or obvious little notes of thanks written on them. Parker had hoped on the first day they'd met that those pictures meant Melody was good at what she did, because Parker and Will were putting their entire future hopes into this woman's hands. Melody had helped them every step of the way, from application to inspection to the final recommendation.

"We've finished the background check and your home inspection impressed Clyde and Sullivan. Clyde isn't easy to impress, either." She gave them a kind smile, settling their file pages on the desk. "Trust me when I say you have a very good chance of being at the top of the list once the state board sees what you can offer."

"There won't be issues because we're both men, will there?" Will asked. He slid Parker a single look, something hiding in them that tugged at Parker's heart. Will was really beginning to want this. Relief unlike anything in recent memory filled Parker. Will's concerns proved it.

"Not from what I've seen, or from your paperwork. You're both in good standing with the city. The family interviews were clean." She made a passive shrug. "My best suggestion is wait a little bit. Let it sink in. I can't make the wheels move any faster, but I do know there are children in the system who will benefit from a loving household." She stood from behind her desk and offered a hand. "I'll be in touch."

"Thank you, very much," Will said, shaking hands. Parker did the same.

Parker was quiet leaving the agency, his thoughts tumbling too rapidly to catch just one. He hid his hands in his pockets, trying to sort through the anguish and impatience he felt.

"Are you okay, cowboy?"

Parker looked up, finding a concerned Will at his shoulder. "I just... I guess I expected something else. It feels like we've come so far and now they're saying go home. Why?"

Will wound a supportive arm around Parker's waist, bringing him close. "Because the final stamp needs to be given. You knew there would be more intense scrutiny given our relationship."

"Doesn't mean I have to like it," he grumbled. He blew out a breath and tried to relax enough to calm the anxiety twisting his gut. "I knew it, though, on some level." He began to walk through the parking lot, oblivious to the traffic surrounding them, the noise of a big city. "I mean, I didn't expect them to drop folders or whatever they use today and say pick one. I know I didn't, but just telling us to go home...to wait." He knew he sounded as sullen and disappointed as he felt.

"You feel like they've already made the choice and it wasn't in our favor," Will said in understanding.

Parker nodded.

Will guided him to the car and leaned him against the fender, searching his face. He moved Parker's cowboy hat up to be able to find his eyes. "Think about how far we've come just since the winter. We're married. You have a good business building. I have a steady business. We have an absolutely amazing, supportive family behind us. We're on the rolls for fostering with the state and we're all but approved by the final board." He brushed through Parker's hair. "Give it time. When it happens, it happens. We may only be fostering for a few weeks to start with. What will you do then?"

"Love them, no matter what."

"Ahh, Parker." Will sighed. "You're going to give your whole heart to any child we care for."

"Is that wrong?" Parker gazed at him, tipping his head, worry building that he could jeopardize their efforts, or flat out ruin them completely. Will's reply eased his fears, but nothing would help his impatience.

"No, it's just going to be painful to watch when they move on. Fostering isn't permanent. We can always look into adoption, but I have to agree with Melody. This will give us a background and record of stability to be considered for a child of our own."

Parker knew that meant better marks and recommendations for when they did decide to go for adoption, but it didn't mean he had to like the methods. Their relationship and his age were both flags. It wasn't a complete block, but it had felt like every move and word was being judged by a different meter.

"We're not going to eat them," Parker said with mild disgust.

Will grinned. "I know that, and honestly, they do too. But the child's welfare will always come first. They want to find a good mix for us." He kissed his lips softly. "I know it's hard to be patient, but in this, we have no choice."

"Patient, huh?" Parker still wasn't thrilled, but at least he wasn't knotted up inside feeling like he'd been kicked and cursed at all over again. "I'll try."

"That's all either of us can do." He nudged Parker with a knee. "Come on. Let's get dinner and then head home."

Parker finally relented and slid away to circle the car. He supposed there really wasn't much choice in the matter. It would happen when it happened, and growling about it wasn't going to do a bit of good. Even if it did make him feel better.

* * * *

The call, when it came three weeks later, caught Parker completely unprepared. The passage of time had gradually lessened the angst and impatience, as one day led to another, life picking up the routine he was familiar with.

He plucked the phone from his belt without looking at the screen. It was common to get inquiries at all times of the day about the lessons and classes he taught, and the horse boarding they offered.

"Vandersoot Training."

"Mr. Vandersoot?"

He leaned against a stall wall, scratching Tank's shoulder. "This is him."

"This is Andrea Ross with the Iowa Department of Human Resources. Do you have time to talk?"

He swallowed, straightening as his heart pounded in a near-panic wave of nerves. "I do." He forcibly calmed his breathing. *No panicking until I know what the call's about.*

"We believe you and Mr. Parkinson are the best candidates for a particular foster that has come up. Is he available to also be on the call?"

He cleared his throat to hide his nerves. "No, I'm sorry. He's at work."

"I see." She sounded hesitant.

"I assure you, we are in agreement and have talked in length about this. If a question comes up that I can't answer, I can call him immediately to return your call."

She took a breath. Parker's skin pricked in the interim.

"Let me give you some of the details. I will need at least individual verbal agreement from both of you to move forward under the circumstances. You'll understand why once you hear the situation."

Parker clicked Tank's stall shut and walked out of the barn so he wouldn't be distracted by a demanding horse looking for treats. "Okay."

"We recently had to take in a set of twins. A boy and a girl, both six years old. We will not separate them. They need a supportive home, stable, with someone constantly available. They need security."

"What happened to their parents?" He feared the worst and what he learned quickly told him that even his worst could be paradise for another.

"Their father is an unknown, unlisted on the birth certificates. Their mother is in jail for drug abuse and child neglect. Unfortunately, there is more in their history. If you and Mr. Parkinson agree, I will fax that to you both to consider."

Those babies. Parker swallowed heavily, keeping his voice even. "I understand. They're fragile."

"Very. They've been in a children's home for several weeks, but after evaluation we feel they need more one on one, direct care. Is that something you can provide?"

"I believe so. I technically work from home and Will is here like any other spouse who works."

"Understandable," she agreed.

"Are either in school yet?"

"They're taking lessons at home for now. School evaluations can be made in the fall if they are still with you. You are both encouraged to ask anything that isn't already compiled in the histories. They are safe in the home where they are, but need a more focused unit. We'd like to have them in a home where they're the only children, at least to start. They may be open to more siblings in the future from what we've seen."

Wow. Parker tipped his head to stare into a cloudless sky. A brother for them? He was jumping ahead and knew it. *Just get them here first.* "So, two, a boy and a girl? We have one room already set up, but can do another in about forty-eight hours."

"They may want to share for a while," she warned him.

"I don't doubt it." Parker was sure there would be fear in another move, in the unknown. If each other was all they had, then... He tapped the heel of his boot at a tuft of grass, thinking. He knew Will wouldn't say no. The only glitch was two, not one. It would be a pinch, but it could be done. With his mind made, he checked his screen with a scanned peek, then asked, "Is this your direct number?"

"It is."

"Let me call Will and have him contact you. He may be with a patient."

"Thank you, Mr. Vandersoot."

"If everything comes together, how long will we have before we meet?"

"Barring any hiccups, seven days."

One week. He released a slow breath. *Wow.* Again.

"I apologize for the short notice, but the sooner we can settle the twins, the better it will be for them, mentally and physically."

There was so much being left unsaid. He knew it. It made it impossible to not want to know what was in their history. He didn't doubt it was going to be ugly. The cautionary truth was in her voice. It was going to be bad. Bad, he knew.

He asked, "You're looking at us because of my history with my father, aren't you?"

He finally heard a smile in her voice, like he'd passed some hidden test. Like maybe he'd proven he did understand the instinctive connection that he already had with these two children who so needed a caring, loving home.

"Actually, yes, among many factors. The counselors believe you will have the ability to understand Micah's apathy and fears. He's not fearful of women right now, but we feel he'd respond more positively with men. He's actually very introverted with everyone. Another change won't be easy for either of them. Again, it's detailed in their files. Please have Mr. Parkinson contact me as soon as he is available."

"When he contacts you, we'll be given their histories to consider?"

"Yes. Please understand, this is a large undertaking, one versus two," she cautioned. "And they are not infants, but young children, already forming ideas and behaviors."

"I understand. I'll call him right now. Expect his phone call within the hour."

"I'll do that. And thank you for taking them into consideration."

"Thank you, Ms. Ross."

He disconnected the call and released a heaved breath as a tremor shook him. He knew from what he'd already been told, he was going to take those babies. His heart ached for what they'd suffered, and probably still suffered, living day to day in the unknown. They might be safe where they are, but being safe didn't necessarily mean they *felt* safe. There was a world of difference between the two. He knew that from personal experience.

Parker might not have had the best childhood. He knew in the end his father had despised him beyond all understanding, but seeing that in his own history, recognizing it, gave him the will and patience to do better. To be a better role model and guide. He understood they were hurting. That he did understand, maybe too well. It made his decision that much easier. He also knew once Will knew what he did, that he would want the same.

He lifted the phone and hit the speed dial for the dental office. "Tammie, is Will busy?"

"No. One sec."

He tucked a hand in a pocket. "Thanks." He was put on hold and waited.

Chapter Five

Will found Parker working in the barn that evening, his silence intense, lost in his own head. He got within feet of his husband without Parker even noticing. Not that he blamed him. Since the phone call with Ms. Ross, he didn't doubt in the least Parker's mind was whirring like a propeller. Will had talked with her for nearly forty-five minutes. He had the psyche analysis and the counselors' recommendations for both children sitting on the table, in an undisturbed folder. He refused to even look at names without Parker at his side.

"Hey, cowboy," he called gently.

Parker straightened from the stall he was cleaning and met Will's gaze. He rested the rake in his hands on a wall and strode right to him. Will opened his arms and held on tight to his frame when they met.

"Anything you need help with?" Will asked. By the bright light illuminating the inside, he knew what the answer was going to be. If it were possible, even the concrete would be sparkling as clean as everything was. It was one of the ways Parker coped with a busy mind. He worked cleaning, scraping, and laying hay for hours.

"No. I'm just staying busy to not think, but that's all I've done since she called." He raised his head from Will's shoulder. "My head is a wreck, making its own monsters for these two, and I'm scared I'm not even going to be close to the monsters they live with already."

"Shh." Will brushed caring fingers through his hair to soothe him. "We'll read what Ms. Ross sent and make an honest decision. We can't go with just our hearts, and we can't ignore their logical needs."

"Knew you were too smart for someone like me," Parker mumbled.

Will hushed him gently. He knew perfectly well how smart Parker was. "I'm just saying we have to be as honest with ourselves and each other as we can be. I can already hear it in your voice what these children mean to you, and you haven't even met them yet."

"Only because I understand the pain."

"I know you do," Will agreed. "And it hurts to think of anyone else living through the same."

Parker nodded, lowering his lashes. "They're babies. Hardly older than Summer."

"Let's finish up in here and go see if this is something we can take on. They may need more than either of us can offer."

Parker reluctantly released Will. It only took another ten minutes to put things in order. The horses would be brought in and fed in a few hours. They had time for dinner.

And for deciding the next step of their lives.

* * * *

"This is heartbreaking," Will said, rereading sections to make sure he had a full grasp. They'd been in the system for a few months already, both just recently turning six. It was like Ms. Ross had said, they were being home schooled, but were showing positive signs to be able to start school in the fall. *If they're still here.*

Ensuring he hadn't missed anything, it was still a difficult situation and rereading wasn't making it any less so. He flipped another page of the detailed reports. It was unbelievable what some people allowed, or in this case inflicted on their own children. The bruises had healed, and they'd put on some weight, but the pictures that were taken at the beginning of their ordeal and put in the files told him so much more than the written facts ever would. Hollow stares filled too-thin faces. The children in the report were almost nothing like the two pictured on the adoption contract. It broke his heart. He wanted to cry for the pair. Life hadn't been kind or fair yet.

Parker stood by the closest window, silent, staring out. His spine was rigid with crossed arms, while he glared at nothing into the darkness.

They'd both already read through everything once. Now they were taking the time to assimilate the information.

"I'm only going to say this now, once, and never again." Parker practically snarled with every word. "I am glad their mother lost custody. She never deserved them. I wouldn't have let her watch a fish."

Will's lips twitched with a smirk, but he wholeheartedly agreed.

"My father was a bastard, abusive and worse, but he kept a roof over my head until..." He gushed a breath. "Well, until he did what he did. By then though, I could survive."

"And you did. You came out a better man than him in every way," Will said. He stood from the chair he was using and walked up behind Parker, encircling his waist.

"Chelsea and Micah need us," Parker whispered. "They need support, family, cousins... Safety."

He eventually relaxed and leaned into Will's front, lowering hands to cover Will's clasped at his waist. Sharing and taking strength.

"Are you sure this doesn't hit too close to home for you? I can tell you're the overprotective papa bear in this," he teased warmly, pushing hair out of the way with his chin to press gentle lips to skin below an ear.

Parker huffed. "Yeah, I guess I am."

"It's going to be a long road, for them and us," Will advised. "We'll all need time to adjust."

Parker motioned he was aware. "Are we really ready? I mean, truthfully?"

Will considered the question. "I think we're crossing paths for a reason. Whether they stay with us or not, I can't guess, but we can give our best to make each morning a better day for them. We can show them the world is not a scary place when you have the right people standing with you."

"God, I love you," Parker choked out, sniffling a little as emotions threatened to overwhelm him. Parker was a big mush ball under the hard working cowboy Will knew and loved. "Can't say it often enough. You are every reason I breathe."

Will turned him around and sipped kisses over tear-damp eyelids. "I love you too, cowboy. More and more every day."

Parker welcomed him when he drew on his lips for a kiss. A sweet tease. Will hoped he never grew tired of those kisses.

"Are we in agreement then? Do we have a second bedroom to put together?"

Parker took a steadying gulp of air, finally meeting Will's gaze with his own—damp, rich with emotion, but clear. "Yes, to both. I know we can at least get the basics in for the second room and let them decorate as they get comfortable."

"I've cleared my early morning so we can call her together." There were still questions to ask, details. But that would come in the morning. The hardest part had been dissected and decided.

Parker melted into his chest.

Will knew no matter what happened, stay or leave, these two would be loved by a lion of a man while they were under their roof.

"The foster isn't for a set time, either," Will pointed out. He didn't want to get Parker's hopes up but with the way Ms. Ross explained it... It left a lot of room for them.

"One day at a time," Parker replied. "It's hard, but I know we need to be realistic about this. It's fostering. And they come first."

Will teased with a tickling tongue to his earlobe a moment later. "How about for tonight, you come first? It's been a while since I got to ride my cowboy into a lather."

Parker groaned then quietly laughed. "You're crazy. Let me get the horses inside and I'll be right there."

"You have thirty minutes," Will informed him.

"I'll be back in twenty," he promised with a lingering caress on Will's ass.

Will shivered and watched Parker walk away until he was out of sight. Something about blue jeans on his man made Will want to pounce on him. Good thing he was out of the room before Will got the chance to follow through with that urge.

* * * *

Parker sauntered up behind Will who was turning down the blankets on the bed. Will had showered and wore a pair of boxers, the kind that molded right to his curves, and that he knew drove Parker nuts.

"Hello, sexy," Parker whispered against his skin.

Will reached a hand backward, found bare skin and moaned. "When'd you get naked?"

"I cheated. I stripped in the other bathroom. It only takes me ten minutes to get the horses inside when there's grain on the menu." He'd also stolen about four minutes to shower himself.

"Cheater." Will chuckled ruefully. "I never remember the evening grain."

He looped arms around Will's middle and kissed his shoulder. "Want you tonight," he said, filled with longing and a hunger to connect.

Will made a rumbled sound that was nearly a quiet growl. Parker smiled, knowing what his husband was thinking, and just what he wanted. He glided a hand downward and teased a nail above the elastic of his boxers. "These need to come off."

Will quickly notched them with his thumbs and pushed them to his thighs. Parker scooted them the rest of the way until they puddled on the floor. He followed their descent, using his tongue to lick a trail down Will's spine until he knelt behind him. Fingers curled at Will's side, revealing his arousal.

Parker licked circles, nibbling and lapping as he teased over skin. Will's breathing hitched and panted depending on where he moved to. Giving a light push to a hip got him to bend over to rest his palms to the bed and Parker nuzzled against the back of his sac between straddled thighs, knowing not going for the sensitive skin just above him was driving Will to distraction. Craving.

"Parker," he pleaded with a whine. Will had no patience when it came to this.

He made him wait a few more minutes, ignoring Will's panted moans.

Will cried out with the first touch, just the tip of his tongue to Will's opening. A long string of sounds were Will's reaction.

Trembles cascaded over Will's frame. Parker loved that he could make Will feel so good, because Will could certainly turn him inside out.

Nipping once with teeth to a dimpled cheek, he stood. "On the bed."

Will scrambled. He landed with a gusted plop then laughed, catching Parker's gaze. "So not fair," he complained. "You know that makes my brain stop working."

Parker grinned, following him onto the bed. "Yep." Will's hand on his calf halted his motions.

"Come up here. I want some fun, too."

Parker swung around on the bed, straddling Will's head. His lashes fluttered when hot breath ghosted over his balls. "Fuck, Will."

"Next," Will mumbled, slurping and licking, repaying Parker for his teasing.

A rough shiver hit Parker's spine when Will roamed scorching lips over his cock, dancing his tongue up and down the shaft as though he hungered to give that delicious torment. Parker knew he loved doing it as much as Parker loved getting it.

He grunted when Will slipped him into his mouth, sucking on the head. Low rumbles of pleasure heightened the intensity. He panted, swept under in a rush as Will scrambled his brain. A light smack on his ass popped him back into the now, telling him in no uncertain terms Will had needs too.

Parker chuckled, enjoying every sound and twitch, then swooped down to engulf Will's length. The surprised grunt was beautiful.

Taking advantage of his position, he slid a wet finger down and eased it inside Will's body. The tremors and whines grew. Will began to huff, sucking harder on Parker's length as his needs multiplied.

Pleasure pulsed for both. Will's inner walls massaged Parker as he increased to two then three fingers. He needed to grab the lube, but damn, it felt so good, the heated pressure and Will's reactions as he coaxed Will's body and rubbed against nerves.

Will was moaning without pause by the time Parker released his cock and his ass. Parker slid over Will, grasping the bottle to kneel between Will's thighs. He rubbed slick around his length, using his thumb to stroke over Will's flexing pucker with the excess.

With an evil smile, he squirted a line down Will's bobbing cock to his balls. The cold liquid made him squirm. "Ready?"

Will reached and clawed at a forearm, his *hurry up and get on with it before I scream* warning.

Parker stroked Will's cock. Will's mouth fell open with a gasp, his eyes sinking shut in bliss. "That's so fucking hot," Parker said. "Sexy." Will moaned, unable to speak with the palm pleasuring him.

Moving closer, he propped Will's legs to line up, bringing them together. There was nothing in Parker's life like loving Will. His lover melted for Parker. He completely understood what he was feeling, how Will was flying because when Will made love to Parker, it was as though he soared above the clouds beneath Will's touch.

Nerves began to spark and hum with each slow thrust. The rush of energy made his heart thunder like a storm against his ribs.

Will's moans thickened. Leaning close, he found Will's lips and kissed him until both were gasping for air. Forehead to forehead, their bodies met, finding the pleasure each yearned for and needed.

Will began to tug on his thickened shaft, the lube easing each pass of his hand. The friction reached Parker and he whimpered, steadily pumping harder. His eyes sank shut and his body took over, muscles straining.

Parker felt the surges, the flex of their meeting bodies and bore down, bracing Will with both hands. The first panted groans filled the room's silence then Parker joined him, filling the tight velvet that caressed his own orgasm from his body with wrenching bliss.

It was several minutes before he tried to move. Of course, the arms holding him in place made it fairly clear there was no hurry to disturb either.

Chapter Six

"Is it normal to be nervous?" Parker asked. They sat on the porch steps waiting for Mr. Jacks, the children's advocacy lawyer, and the twins. Parker had barely slept the night before. He'd been up well before the alarm and in the barn, trying to work through some of the anxiety crawling through him for the coming meeting. He hadn't succeeded as much as he'd hoped.

Will one-arm hugged him around the shoulders. "I would think so. I am too, honestly."

Parker stared at him in disbelief from under the brim of his hat. "I don't see it."

Will only smiled. Parker saw none of his own fears mirrored in Will.

This was a huge undertaking. He knew that. The bedrooms were ready, if a little sparse. They wanted to let the kids feel welcome, give them the chance to make each room what they wanted it to be. There was some color, enough to welcome them, but Parker hoped the twins grew into the rooms, for however long they were there. He wanted them to know they were wanted.

The second bedroom meant Parker's home office had to be moved down the hall to the smallest side room, but he was fine with that. He'd move into the kitchen if he had to for these two kids.

Lost in his thoughts, the sound of vehicle tires turning off the road and onto the drive made him jerk his head up. He swallowed and stood slowly. Will mimicked him.

"Relax," Will whispered. "I'm right here with you."

Parker twisted toward Will and kissed his temple. "Lost without you."

Will sighed, simply touching hand to hand to walk a few steps together off the porch to wait.

The van rolled to a stop. The driver door opened. "Mr. Parkinson, Mr. Vandersoot." Mr. Jacks came forward and shook hands. "Thank you for being here." After that, the lawyer turned and opened the closest side door with a button. "Micah, Chelsea, you can come out and take a look," he told the pair gently.

Micah was cautious, slow to remove his seatbelt and slide to the floorboard. He inched to the van opening and Mr. Jacks helped him to the ground. Chelsea followed him until they both stood side by side. Micah reached for his sister's hand. Chelsea clutched a beat up blue bear to her chest.

Wide, brown eyes stared in duplicate. Neither said a peep.

"We're very glad you could be here with us," Will said in warm greeting. "I'm Will and this is Parker."

Parker noted when both looked at each man when Will gave their names.

"Are you a cowboy?" Chelsea asked, blatantly fixated on his hat.

Parker's gaze followed hers, looking through his lashes, landing on the front brim of his hat before answering. "I am."

"Do you have horses?" She seemed to be the more outgoing of the two and Parker was going to let them take the pace they were most comfortable with.

"Almost ten right now. Would you like to see one or two?"

"Yes, please!" Her little face lit up. Micah didn't say a word, but he didn't balk when Chelsea tugged on him to follow.

"The barn is around back." Parker smiled easily. "Stay close though, okay?"

She nodded vigorously, following Parker next.

* * * *

Will watched Parker wind those kids close and without even letting them know they'd been caught.

"He's good," Mr. Jacks said, keeping his voice lowered when Parker and the twins were a few paces ahead.

"He's a big kid at heart, but more mature than some grandparents I see."

Mr. Jacks nodded sagely. "It's good to see. They ate on the way here, but will be hungry for dinner soon."

"Will you be staying?"

"Not that long. I'll make sure they're comfortable, do the inspection, and then I'll go so you can have some time to get acquainted. You can expect phone calls in the morning."

Will knew what he was talking about. The spot-check inspections and interviews. Some would be scheduled, but the ones that weren't... They'd deal with those as they happened. They needed to get today under their belts. "I just don't want to traumatize them any more than they have been, scheduled regulations or not."

"I'm glad to hear that. I'm Finn, Finnigan."

"Irish, huh?"

"So far back, it's a myth," he quipped.

Will snorted a laugh.

"The less tense you are, the easier it is on the kids to relax," he mentioned with a knowing smile.

"Sneaky, but I understand. We're both thrilled to have them here." Will strolled with his hands in his pockets next to Finn, trailing the other three to find them in the barn, talking quietly.

They watched Parker crouch beside the pair and point, explaining the barn, the animals, and probably already laying a few ground rules. It was no less than he'd done with Summer.

It was taking a few minutes, but even Micah was starting to show some interest, listening, even if he wasn't speaking. He still clutched Chelsea's hand. Will wanted to hug both and never let them be hurt again.

They were a beautiful pair of kids. Black hair, cut short, though a little longer on Chelsea. They wore jeans and T-shirts, and scuffed sneakers. "Do they have any clothing with them?"

"I have a suitcase for each in the van. It's what they've accumulated since going into the system. It's not much, but it's theirs."

"Even the littlest that they are familiar with will give them something of their own while they settle in here."

"They're donated," Finn said privately. "A charity that collects clothes and small things for the kids and then puts them in an age appropriate bag. When we have to move them, it gives the kids a sense of ownership. Something that is theirs and only theirs. It's not unusual for the clothes that they do get to be hand-me-downs or donated cast offs. More often than not, all they have goes in a trash bag to wherever they go. It's heartbreaking."

Will was shocked at the revelation. "A trash bag?" His heart bled inside for what all the kids had to deal with.

Finn nodded. "Neither has much right now," he cautioned.

"We'll be taking care of that tomorrow." Will was firm on that.

Parker stood and asked the kids a question. Chelsea seemed excited, Micah less so, but at least willing to go along with whatever his sister was doing.

Leading the way, he came to where Will and Finn were waiting. "They're excited about seeing their rooms."

"Well, let's go show them," Will piped up. The group trooped from the barn to the rear door of the home. Will noticed Finn was standing aside, letting the kids take in the house that they would be calling home for the foreseeable future.

Will opened the first door in the hallway. "Micah, this is your room."

Big brown eyes all but popped out of his head. "Mine?" he whispered.

"Yep. All yours. Go ahead." Will turned on the light to let him see what waited for him.

The neatly made bed had a soft comforter with clouds on it and a fluffy pillow on top. The walls were painted a very pale blue to match. The furniture was whitewashed, with a small dresser beside a kid-sized table and chair.

"What is that on the bed?" Finn asked, giving him a nudge to go into the room to see for himself.

Cautiously, Micah released Chelsea and approached the bed. Climbing up to reach, he pulled the stuffed horse toward him.

When he turned with it in his hands, a question in his eyes, Parker told him, "It's yours, Micah. We wanted you to know you are wanted, and we already think you're both special."

"Do I have a room?" Chelsea asked, peering up at them expectantly.

Will laughed warmly. "You know, I think you do." He scooted out the door and went down the hall to the next doorway, opening it to let them all into that one. "I bet this is Chelsea's room," he stated.

Chelsea skipped beside him and came to a halt, gaping with her mouth as wide as Micah's eyes had been.

"Do you like it?" Parker asked.

Parker had put a lot of energy and thought into the rooms, especially since they only had a week to get the second one put together. The two rooms had been a project of love.

"I get to keep it?" she asked nearly reverently.

"It's your room," Parker answered.

The bed was covered with a light purple comforter with colorful pictures of candy lollipops near the foot end, like a lollipop forest. The walls were painted in curvy vertical waves with colors that matched the lollipops. The furniture was white, the same as Micah's, but instead of a table and chair, she had a mini chalkboard easel.

"I think there's a gift for you too," Will pointed out.

Chelsea hopped over to the bed and bounced up to reach. She squealed, then spun, clutching her own horse. "Mr. Bear has a friend!" She squeezed them both into her chest.

Will nodded. "He sure does."

She snuggled the horse close.

"Why don't we get their things and they can put away their clothes in their dressers," Will suggested. He felt ready to burst, seeing both kids so happy. Even Micah's stoic silence couldn't hide the way he clutched his horse to himself.

Chelsea scurried from the room, grabbing Micah's hand on the way. They started comparing horses. The two toys were nearly identical, but to avoid confusion, Chelsea's had socks on its legs. Like the twins, only not. How Parker had come to that conclusion amazed Will, because it looked like he was on the money. They seemed to like the differences as much as the similarities.

He and Parker led the way through the home, with Mr. Jacks bringing up the rear. Will knew that once the initial fear and excitement had abated, they'd take the time to show them the house. He was just as sure dinner would soon be on the menu for the two kids.

They ran out the front door for the van, slapping the side wall in a tie. The rear door clicked and slowly began to rise.

"Micah, Chelsea," Finn called. He tugged the miniature cases out, one in each hand. "Here are your clothes. You're both going to be very happy here."

Will saw the connection happen instantly. They were being left...somewhere. Again.

"Who wants dinner? I hear hotdogs are on the menu." Will's announcement barely made either look his direction. Chelsea's lower lip began to wobble. She and Micah huddled together, bolstering the other without so much as attempting to take the offered cases.

"Hey," Parker cajoled, getting down on their level again. "We know you're nervous. So are we. But we know something you don't."

Chelsea gave him a disbelieving scowl. "What?" Like she was only waiting for the next upheaval.

"We know that tomorrow morning, we'll all be sitting down to breakfast, that tomorrow night, you'll get to cuddle up in bed for stories, and that the day after that we'll be doing it again."

"And the day after that?" she pressed.

"And every day after that." Parker emphasized it with a head nod. "We know you were at your between house before, but we're not a between house. We're going to take care of you, the both of you." He shared a look with a silent, evasive Micah. "And you want to know something?"

"What?" A little less petulant.

"We promise to show you every day that we want you here. But this is the deal, you have to give us a chance, too, okay?"

Chelsea seemed to consider it, sharing a long, silent communicative moment with Micah. She finally faced Parker and nodded. "So we're staying here?"

"Staying as in going to be living with us as your foster parents. Not caregivers, not babysitters, but foster parents. Both of you."

She hugged on her horse and Mr. Bear. "Can we still have hotdogs?"

The littleness of her voice almost killed Will. He hoped to never hear that aching sound in her voice again.

"Of course," Parker said, smiling broadly. "Let's get your things put away, in your rooms, and get cleaned up." He stood straight. "Before we go, you need to tell Mr. Jacks thank you for bringing you here."

"Thank you, Mr. Jacks," they both chimed, albeit one was decidedly quieter than the other.

"You're very welcome kids." He reached and shook hands in farewell. "We'll be in touch, and good luck."

Will and Parker guided the kids toward the front of the house. It surprised Will when Chelsea turned and waved at the van. A quick double honk was her reply and then the van was on the road and disappearing.

Will held the door open for them all. "I'll meet you in the kitchen."

Parker replied with a silent love you on his lips.

Chapter Seven

Parker adjusted Micah on the car seat booster. "All set?" Parker asked the youngster. He nodded. Micah still wasn't talking much. It worried Parker, but he knew the boy just needed time. The twins had barely been with them a week. "Chelsea?"

She tugged on her belt. "I'm in!"

"Good girl," Parker said. "Let's go get some food!"

"Yippeee!" Chelsea called.

She was so full of life, Parker didn't think he'd stopped smiling since they'd arrived.

"Everyone in?" Will stood across the car, his door open on the other side.

"We're set. Off to Uncle Brice and Uncle Jake's."

"And pancakes," Will added. He winked for Parker. Will totally knew his pancake addiction was all Jake's fault.

Parker tapped Micah's foot and shut the door. He was a little nervous for the kids. He didn't think they had an inkling of the mayhem they were about to encounter. Summer was excited to finally get to meet them, as were the rest of the family. Will and Parker both wanted to take some time to give the kids a chance to feel some level of comfort and safety in their new home before siccing the rest of the family on them.

And as far as he knew, no one was immune to Jake's pancakes. He hoped they helped break down the walls Micah still hid behind.

It took only a few minutes to drive across Jasper to Brice's cozy home. It was getting to be a bit of a squeeze for them to all gather in the smaller house, but no one complained. It felt like family to Parker, and he cherished every Sunday breakfast no matter whose house it was at–including their own.

Now that would be an adventure for the kids. He couldn't wait.

He rolled to a stop behind Jeannie's SUV. "Huh, where's Tucker?" His big, brown dually truck was definitely missing.

"You don't think Vivian popped, do you?"

Parker grinned. "Only one way to find out. Let's go see if we have a nephew." Brice would be the man to know since Tucker was Brice's older brother. Parker slipped off his belt and opened the door to reach for Micah's. "All right, let's go get some pancakes," he said, enticing the now quieter kids out of their boosters. They were watching the house with a nervous expectancy. He offered a hand for Micah and his gut trembled when the boy took it with hardly a hiccup. He swallowed the bubble of emotion. Maybe new situations were what Micah needed to learn he could rely on someone besides Chelsea. Guiding him around the car, they met up with Will and Chelsea, also holding hands. Parker's heart fluttered again.

He totally loved these kids.

"We're not being left again, are we?" Chelsea asked, stopping them all cold.

Will's steps stuttered and he latched onto Parker's gaze. He was sure the pain he felt was what he was looking at in Will.

"No." Will crouched low and spoke to both kids. "We're here to eat. The rest of our family wants to meet you. There is a young girl in that house who has probably been driving her mothers crazy wanting to meet you." He searched both of the kids in front of them. "You're here with us, and you'll both be going home with us. I promise that."

"Promise?" she demanded with a tremulous bravado.

"Completely." He squeezed her hand and with a final head nod at both, he straightened to his feet.

Parker took a slow breath. It was these moments that cut him to the quick. At their age, to be worried about what each day would bring. Whether they'd be dropped off with yet another adult, another house, another move that left them with no sense of home, of stability. That was no way to live, no way to grow up.

Will tapped on the front door and within seconds it opened to a beaming Brice. He swung the door wide for them to go in. "We almost had to tie Summer down. She's so excited to meet them both," he said for Will's and Parker's benefit. Brice smiled for the kids. "I'm Brice."

Will looked down and nodded with a smile in encouragement.

"Hello. I'm Chelsea." She bravely offered a hand and Brice shook it.

"Lovely to meet you." He turned toward Micah. "And this must be Micah."

He hid in Parker's hip, clutching his hand harder.

"Give him time," Parker suggested, soothing Micah with a stroking hand on his hair.

"All the time in the world," Brice said kindly. "Is it safe to let out the wild one?"

"Sure," Will answered. "Might be exactly what they need."

"Okay, but you've been warned," Brice offered in lowered tones. "Summer! They're here!"

A squeal filled the house, bringing the chatter to a near standstill in its wake. Summer tore into the front room from somewhere and came to a skidding halt at Brice's leg. Her eyes went saucer wide, staring at the twins.

And she didn't say a word.

"I hope her mothers are seeing this. She's speechless." Will laughed deeply.

"It's being noted," Wanda piped up from the kitchen, watching the scene from the doorway.

"Hi," Chelsea whispered, staring just as hard right back at her.

"Hi. Want to play?"

Chelsea nodded and went to step away, freezing in her tracks. She sought upward. "May we, Will?"

"Of course, and thank you for being so polite to ask."

She smiled like she'd found the key to a candy store. Parker glanced down. "You can too, Micah. We'll let you know when breakfast is ready."

Slowly, he disentangled hands, following after an already chattering Summer and Chelsea.

"They're adorable. Six, right?"

Parker hung his hat by the door. "A hair over six. Their birthday was in May."

"Where are Tucker and Vivian?" Will asked following Parker and Brice toward the crowded kitchen where the smell of hot syrup and maple sausage filled the air. Parker's stomach rumbled in appreciation. The house was packed so they only got as far as the kitchen entry, but it was plenty close enough to see the laden counters and set table. His mouth watered. Yeah, he had a soft spot for pancakes. *So sue me.*

"She went into labor about three this morning." Brice was as proud as a new uncle could be.

"Ha!" Will crowed. "I knew it!"

"Christopher Jacob was born at seven forty-three this morning. I have all the stats on the board in the office. It was the closest thing to write on at that hour."

"Congratulations!" Parker popped him playfully on the back with a hand. Parker and Will both chuckled at his vocal *oomph.*

Ian appeared from around Jake's other side with a mug of coffee for each. "How's the new world of children underfoot for you?"

"It's been amazing," Parker said, accepting the hot brew.

More mugs were handed around. Will blew on his. "Best part of breakfast, I swear." He sighed after taking a long sip. It was Ian's job to make the coffee for Sunday mornings. He'd earned that job honestly.

"How are they settling in?" Ian asked.

"Chelsea's far more outgoing. I don't think Micah is really shy or overly quiet. I think he's a thinker," Will said. "He's very exact about some things."

"I noticed that too," Parker agreed. They both turned as children's laughter filled the house. "And then there's that." He grinned indulgently. "I knew Summer would be good for them. Nothing holds her down."

Jeannie came to stand with them. "Will they be going to school here?"

"If they're still here, we're planning on it. They should be capable to go into first grade, unless something happens. Then they'll only be a year off from the majority, at the most."

"If?" Ian asked.

"We're still only a temporary foster," Parker informed them.

Will shared a questioning look with Parker and he nodded in answer. He knew what Will was asking.

"If all goes well, we want to petition to adopt at the end of the summer, but the kids need time. So do we." Will kept his voice lowered for privacy, not that any of the kids could hear him over their own squeals and laughter.

"They've been here a week and you're already considering adoption?" Ian wasn't exactly shocked, but he studied Parker closely. "Are you sure, Parker?"

"Since the moment I saw them," he admitted. "I love them. I love you guys. They need something we can give them. A family."

Ian raised a hand as though to brush over his nose while looking away, clearing his throat before meeting Parker's gaze. The pride in his gaze was unmistakable. "That means a lot."

"I had great role models," he said, meaning it. "Speaking of, where is Caleb?"

"In the office, sharing the baby news with the rest of the family. And probably inviting everyone down for a barbecue." Ian rolled his eyes.

"You know you love grilling, and didn't Caleb just buy you a fancy new pit for your anniversary this year?" Jeannie teasingly poked him in the shoulder.

Ian pursed his lips, attempting to hide his smiles, and failing. "Yeah."

"Why don't you go get Caleb off the phone with Jessie, or whichever one he's talking to," Jake said loud enough to be overheard. "It's as ready as it can be."

"I'll go," Jeannie offered. "I'll get the kids to wash up."

Taking a few minutes, Parker nudged Will out of the kitchen doorway into the open living room and stole a quick kiss. "Love you," he murmured against coffee warmed lips.

Will said before Parker straightened, "We're going to have an awesome family."

"We already do," Parker agreed.

* * * *

Will turned over in bed Sunday night and blinked. "Did you hear that?" he mumbled. The dark bedroom made it hard to focus. His internal clock was clamoring that it was way too early to be awake. He had to agree.

Parker made a low grumbled moan. "I think so." He hefted to an elbow, trying to get his bearings.

"Let me check the kids."

"I'll check the doors," Parker offered.

They slipped from the bed and went different ways in the hall. Will peeked in Micah's room, and frowned. Micah's bed was empty, the covers pushed back. Hopefully, he was only one room down.

Neither of the kids had been restless since their arrival, but Will knew anything could disturb their sleep enough to want to cuddle with the other. They'd had huge changes in their lives in the last few months, and today had been exhausting and crazy. Summer had run them ragged before and after breakfast, playing in the front yard after everyone was as full as ticks, running off all the food they'd eaten, from Jake's pancakes to hash browns. Proof they were growing kids, they'd eaten like horses. The three of them had a lot of the adults laughing at their antics, Will and Parker among them. It was a good Sunday.

Parker was right. They had an amazing family.

Walking down the hall to Chelsea's room, he found her sound asleep. And alone.

"Oh, that's not good," he whispered.

Parker came up behind him. "I need to get shoes. The back door was cracked open."

"Micah's not in bed."

Parker spun and trotted for the bedroom to slip on sneakers and a T-shirt with the sleep bottoms he already wore. He scurried to the kitchen for a flashlight with Will on his heels.

"I'll stay here in case he comes back."

Parker nodded and slipped out of the house, using the flashlight to light his way to the barn. It was the logical place to start. Will turned on the kitchen light, gnawing on his bottom lip. When minutes dragged, he crossed his arms and watched the darkness like a hawk through one of the back windows.

* * * *

Parker waved the flashlight in an arc, hunting across the ground and into shadows. "Micah?" he called, not too loudly. He didn't want to startle him if he were scared or panicky. "Hey, guy, it's Parker. Where'd you go?"

As he neared the barn, he spotted the side door hanging ajar. "Should've been my own," he mused aloud. *Just like when I was a kid.*

He slipped into the barn, hearing the shifting of sleepy horses. He didn't want to turn on the overhead lights and wake up everyone. "Micah? Are you in here?"

A rustle that didn't sound like a horse drew him deeper into the barn. He swept the stalls broadly, checking each horse as he neared. Both kids had been warned profusely about going into stalls with the horses. It would be too easy for a horse to step on one. His heart thundered as he cleared stall after stall and still didn't see the boy. "Micah?"

More rustles drew him to the empty stall on the other side of Tank.

He also heard a meow.

Parker stopped at the wall to gaze into the corner at the boy in race car pajamas curled up in the hay with a cat. And a handful of very small, newborn kittens that he could see through the hay. He shook his head then turned off the flashlight. Everyone knew he was there now.

"What did you find?" Parker asked gently to not startle the boy or mama kitty. She was keeping an eye on Micah, but didn't appear too concerned with his presence.

"Kittens," Micah whispered. He didn't touch. His hands were folded up under his cheek as he watched with unblinking attention while the mama cat tongue-bathed the fuzzy lumps.

Parker knew the cat had been around, but hadn't realized she was that pregnant. It seemed their barn had been reserved as birthing central.

Parker lowered and sat cross-legged on the ground at the gate. "You gave us a scare," he said. "You should be in bed asleep."

"I was worried about Tinker."

So she has a name already, huh? "Well, it looks like she is going to be just fine."

"Are you going to make her go away?"

Parker's spine stiffened. It was asked with a child's innocence but he sincerely doubted it was that simple.

"I don't see why we would," he answered honestly. "We might have the vet check her, make sure she's healthy." *Get her fixed.* He wasn't against barn cats. He didn't want a feral colony taking over. "Especially since she's already got a name, seems like she's got a home, too."

Micah slid a look in his direction then returned to watching the cat. "I have a name."

Damn, he's smart. He thought about the best way to answer the veiled meaning in the question. "Yes, you do. And I know Will and I don't want you or Chelsea going anywhere, either." He knew it wasn't that easy, but the connection was important to Micah. It was also the most the boy had spoken to anyone since he'd moved in. It proved Parker right. The boy was intelligent beyond his six years. He knew what it meant to be removed, what it meant to not have a home that he could trust. That almost broke Parker's heart.

"Why don't we let Tinker take care of her babies for tonight, and get you back into bed? I know Will is worried about you, too."

"He is?" he asked a little hesitantly, avoiding Parker's scrutiny now. Like he knew he'd been bad, and was waiting for the fallout.

"We both were, but now that I've found you, we just have to let Will know you're okay." He waited for Micah's next move. "He's waiting inside for the both of us."

"Am I going to be spanked?"

Parker twitched, hiding it by gripping the flashlight. "Never, Micah." His voice was rough with memories of his own. Too many beatings that he would never forget. "We will never raise a hand to you or your sister. You know you shouldn't have been out here, and you know you did wrong. You'll make better choices as you get older because of what you learn now." He drew a careful breath. So many things his father had done that he'd never do, not in a million years. "When is a better time to come see Tinker?"

"During the day," he mumbled.

That almost killed the boy to admit, but Parker didn't let his expression change. "That's right. So let's go get both of us to bed, okay?" He offered a hand and waited.

Slowly, Micah inched from his balled up spot and reached for Parker's hand. He hefted the child into his chest and let out a quiet sigh of relief when he wrapped both hands around Parker's neck. "Hang on," he cautioned before he stood.

He carried Micah through the barn, securing the door on his way out. Using the flashlight, he made a straight line for the back door. Will must have been watching from the window because the door glided open as they approached.

"Everything okay?" Will asked.

Parker nodded. "Tell Will you're sorry for making him worry. You need to accept your mistakes."

Micah flipped from where he rested on Parker's shoulder to stare at Will. "I'm sorry, Will. I won't do it again."

Will roughed his hair. "Glad you're okay. You gave us a good scare."

"Back to bed with you." Parker carried him to his bedroom and let him get settled on his bed. "See you in a few hours." He started to rise, then on impulse, leaned close and kissed the boy's forehead. "We'll see how Tinker's doing in the morning, okay?"

Micah almost beamed, but it was broken by a yawn. "'Night Parker."

Parker tucked him in and then trailed Will to the bedroom. It only took a few minutes to inform his husband about their newest family members, and the reason behind Micah's nighttime adventure.

"How do we help him feel safe?" Will asked after a few minutes of quiet when they'd both settled down again.

"Do what we're doing. It'll take time, and showing them both that we mean what we say."

"So I guess that means we have a barn cat now, huh?"

"And kittens," Parker joked. He snuggled into Will's back. "Go to sleep. The alarm goes off in three and a half hours."

Will groaned but didn't argue.

Chapter Eight

Tinker was probably the most spoiled rotten barn cat in history. She soon not only had her own stall but blankets and a small box to hide in. Micah checked on her several times a day, making sure she had food and water. Parker kept an eye on Micah, who kept an eye on the feline family. Both kids kept a respectable distance and never once tried to pet the kittens. Parker didn't understand the power of that restraint. He'd have been all over them at that age.

Watching the kids during a lull with the barn work, he answered his vibrating phone. "Vandersoot Training."

"Uh, Parker?"

"This is him."

A throat cleared. "This is Kyle...Kyle Steppen. Don't hang up!" he blurted before Parker could get mad enough to do something impolite. "Please."

Parker took a few steps away from the kids to be able to listen and talk a little freer. "What do you want?"

"Look, I'm just going to tell you. I need your help."

"You're fu—" He caught himself, bit it off, and tried again. "You're kidding me? What on earth could I possibly help you with?" His father's old foreman had absolutely nothing Parker could need or want. He was positive it was a mutual situation.

"I don't know who else to ask."

74

"I haven't been on that ranch in over four years, almost five. You have it all."

"I know." He let out a breath. "I'm working it...alone. Everyone left."

Parker managed to not snicker at the man's predicaments. "Can't help you there." But he felt no sympathy for the man either.

After the belittling and demeaning outbursts Kyle had made at his father's funeral toward Parker and his friends, he'd known Kyle's days were numbered. He'd rarely seen anyone as hate-filled or blindly hero worshiping as Kyle had been that day. His behavior coincided with what Travis had said the other man had been doing, causing them problems all over the Galveston area as well. It looked like his attitude and his opinions had caught up with him if his field crew had left him high and dry.

"Chet screwed me over," he finally admitted.

That sounded more like something Parker's father would do. "What do you mean?"

"He gave me the ranch because it's losing money. It's so far in the hole, I could shake hands with China. I don't know if he did it because he thought I could save it, or to protect you, but I'm fighting tooth and nail to not lose it all and everyone's quit on me."

"Why would he do any of that?" Parker asked. "Dad didn't have a kind bone in his body."

"I was in love with your dad," Kyle whispered. Whether that was shame in his voice or not, Parker couldn't tell but it sure sounded like it. "I would have done anything he'd asked, including save the ranch. I can't."

"Did he know?"

"No," he replied, sounding much smaller on the other end.

"Wait." He pushed his hat up with a stiff finger and ran a hand down his face. "You were sleeping with my dad, weren't you?"

Utter silence told him the answer. He growled low in his throat and stalked to the opposite end of the barn, away from young ears. No way did he want the kids to hear any of this. "So you were fucking my father, gloating at the way he treated his own son, and now you want my help to save your fucking ass?" He was breathing hard. "You've got fucking balls, Kyle."

He disconnected the line without a second's thought then leaned his head to crossed arms on the closest stall wall, fighting to twist his world into some sense of normal.

Fuck it. When had his world ever been normal? Kyle and Dad. He swallowed down the disgust burning his throat. That explained so much, though. Parker had been blindsided when his father had died of a heart attack almost a year ago, and then by the news that he'd rewritten his last will. He'd given the entire ranch enterprise to Kyle.

Now he knew why.

He drew slow breaths through his nose, easing the roil of his stomach. He thought he could honestly retch over that revelation. Kyle was roughly twelve years older than Parker. That meant there was more than thirty years between—

He shuddered. It wasn't a conscious reaction. Parker had never thought one way or another about age gaps with couples. What made them happy, go for it.

Parker had been a later in life baby to begin with, his dad being in his forties when he'd been born. He'd finally found a woman to marry and had him.

Parker's mother had divorced him and given up all rights. He knew now that she had escaped, and didn't blame her one little bit after living under that man's roof for almost seventeen years. He'd been a mean-assed fucker, abusive and uncaring. The only thing that had mattered to Chet Vandersoot had been his bull riding legacy. When he'd died, there wasn't even that any longer for him to cling to.

But Kyle and his dad? Yeah. That crossed the line right into creepy-ville. He didn't care what had brought them together. He didn't doubt in the least either that Chet had used him. There had been no such thing as affection in Chet's selfish soul.

It also explained a hell of a lot more about why Kyle got the ranch. If it was as broke as Kyle seemed to think, then Chet didn't give him the property to save. He gave it to him to sink his ass. A final blow for liking men. Against his own lover.

"You have no idea just how evil and deceitful my dad could be, Kyle," he muttered. *And you played right into his hands.*

Probably gave Chet everything he asked for without truly getting one thing in return.

Knowing that almost...*almost*...made him feel sorry for the other man.

A small tug on his shirt made him clear his features in a hurry to look down. "Yes, ma'am?"

"I'm hungry," Chelsea said.

Parker smiled. This he knew. This he understood. Kyle and Texas were far away and would never be a part of his life again. "You are, huh?" he said with a light laugh. She nodded. "Is Micah?"

She looked toward the stall were the mama cat and kittens were living. "He said he was."

"I think we can do something about lunch. It is about that time." He clipped the phone into its case to call for Micah. "Lunchtime, buddy."

He scooted from the hay and found his feet, trotting over to Chelsea. Parker waited for him to grab Chelsea's hand but was happily taken by surprise when he didn't. Micah watched him, patiently. Seeing the boy bloom into his confidence warmed Parker deep in his chest.

"Let's go see what we can cook up in the kitchen." He offered his hands and each child took one. Their small palms in his were the best medicine to wipe the entire previous conversation from his thoughts.

"Go wash up to eat," he told them once they were inside. They scampered down the hallway, making just as much noise on the return. He wasn't any type of a cook, but he could manage hotdogs with carrot sticks and macaroni and cheese without too much trouble. After getting both kids a half full glass of chocolate milk, he slapped a sandwich together for himself. They all took a seat at the kitchen table and started eating.

They were rambunctious while they ate, using the carrots to make walrus tusks and seeing how large a chocolate mustache they could get. It was good to see them laughing and playing. It was such a positive change from the subdued first few days after they'd arrived a little more than two weeks ago.

"You two ready to help me with Summer's riding lesson?" he asked when they were finished eating.

"Yes!" they both chimed.

"Okay, go clean up and wash your faces. I still see chocolate milk, and then we'll get started."

They quickly gathered their lunch plates to put in the sink and raced for the bathroom to attempt to wash up again.

* * * *

Parker shooed the kids out to the living room after dinner that night, letting them watch a Disney movie they both liked until bedtime. It wasn't an every night thing, but he needed a few minutes to talk with Will about the phone call he'd gotten earlier in the day. They were discussing things quietly after the cleanup had been finished for the evening.

Parker had already regaled him with the entirety and the man's reasoning for making the call to begin with.

"I really don't know what kind of help he thinks you can give him," Will said, leaning against the counter.

"I don't know either, to be honest," Parker agreed. "I can't replace the men who've left him, even if I wanted to." He huffed, crossing his arms to lean beside Will at the counter. Both were keeping an ear and a watchful eye toward the living room, but so far, all Parker had heard were childish giggles coinciding with music.

"How bad off do you think the ranch is?"

"Well, Mrs. Adams, the lawyer who handled the will, said something at the last meeting I had with her about taxes." Parker glanced over to Will at his shoulder. "It could be Dad was gut deep in back taxes and never told anyone."

"That's possible." Will's brow furrowed. "Kyle doesn't think you have some way to rescue the ranch, does he?"

Parker out and out snorted at that idea. "Even if I could, I wouldn't. I lost my home the day Dad kicked

79

me out. That ranch has nothing for me. He got rid of me, my horse, and all of my belongings." He lowered his voice when he realized the old bitterness was making him snarl a bit. "He completely erased me from living there, from being his son. I needed Caleb and Ian's help just to get my social security card and birth certificate again. For all I know, he burned them."

Will faced him, touching his cheek lightly. "I know, sweetheart."

Parker released a slow, controlled breath. "Sorry."

"No need to apologize. You have every right to be angry over what he put you through."

Parker lowered his gaze, dropping his arms at the same time. Will's understanding and patience were part of why he loved his man so much. "Yeah, but it's past, and can't change what's been. Being angry now..." Another slow breath and he lifted his chin to find Will's kind and worried gaze searching him. "A waste of energy."

Will hugged him at the waist and Parker returned it, resting his head on Will's shoulder. "Whatever got into Kyle's head, I don't know. I don't know what he thought I could help him with, either." He snickered. "I hung up on him before he got the chance."

Straightening without letting him go, Will asked, "Do you really think his decision to leave it to Kyle had to do with their...physical relationship?"

"I think so, but I'm sure my father's thinking was it was a final blow to Kyle. Legally he was just the logical person to get it. You didn't know my dad," he said quietly. "He really wasn't the kind to use the emotional reasoning we see as his own. What we see, now that I know how he used Kyle; it's obvious. He wouldn't have given him the ranch because he cared."

In fact, he was sure his father had been completely, willfully blind to Kyle's feelings for him. There was zero emotional purpose to leaving him the ranch other than simply *not* leaving it to Parker.

"I don't say it often, but your father was a dick."

Parker choked on his laughter. "Thank God I like your parents."

Will chuckled too. "Yeah. They like you too. They know I found a good cowboy."

Parker went to mush inside. He shifted enough to kiss Will on the neck. "Love you."

"Love my cowboy," Will told him huskily.

A few more minutes of silent promises for later were brought to an eventual end by another bout of childish giggles.

"Guess we better go make sure they're only watching the movie," Parker advised.

"You watch them. I'll be watching you." Will nipped at Parker's lower lip, letting him go before Parker could gather himself to retaliate.

Chapter Nine

Will was finishing up his last patient of the afternoon a couple of weeks later when children's voices drifted from the front of the office. He tipped his head until he heard Parker as well, then he focused on his patient. "Okay. Almost done."

A verbal agreement with a head nod was his answer from Todd. He didn't try to talk with Will's fingers holding the replacement crown in place for him.

Will did a final check on the crown setting, then sat straight. "The cement will hold, but give it at least an hour to an hour and a half to cure. No eating or drinking." Will removed the paper bib and wadded it up to toss in the trash bin.

"I knew as soon as I bit down, whatever was in that burger was going to cause me trouble." Todd shook his head ruefully. "Probably a bone chip."

"It happens." Will stood and let him walk from the exam room toward the front.

Will walked through the interior door to the waiting room.

"Will!" Two voices chimed in giddy unison.

"Parker took us for ice cream at Lucy's!" Chelsea exclaimed.

Will got down on a knee and hugged both of the kids. "He did?" he asked, smiling broadly. He stood to his feet.

"Yep. Took Tinker and family to the vet for a checkup. We need to pick them up in a few minutes." Parker stood between the kids. "Thought ice cream would help pass the time. The vet said once she's weaned the kittens, we can take her in to get fixed."

Will was fine with that. Neither really wanted an army of cats.

"Kittens?" Todd asked.

"We have four!" Chelsea piped up.

"Are you going to be looking for homes for them?"

"For the kittens? Yes. Tinker will be plenty spoiled," Parker said. "Micah here takes great care of her." He curled a hand over Micah's shoulder, who beamed at the praise, standing taller.

Todd slid his checkbook into a rear pocket after paying Tammie for the day's visit. "I'd love to come take a look. My wife's birthday is coming up and she's been hinting at a friend for Bernie. We usually adopt from the shelters, but this would be an even better surprise."

"You're welcome to come any time. I'm usually there with these two." Parker motioned toward the twins.

"I don't remember you having children," Todd said to Will, curiosity in his tone.

"We're fostering," Will supplied.

"So it's temporary?"

"For now," Will replied. And as soon as he said it, he realized how the twins heard him. He knew how sensitive Micah's sense of stability was. "But we're not letting them go anytime soon," he rushed to add. Unfortunately, with the way the pair crowded Parker's legs, the damage was done. Their little faces had shut down, both avoiding looking at him now.

All he could muster was a tight smile for Parker. "Why don't you guys go get Tinker and I'll meet you at the house?"

"Okay." Parker met his gaze. "It'll be all right," he whispered as the three of them turned to leave.

"I hope so." He let out a breath when the door swung shut behind them.

"Did I say something wrong?" Todd asked.

"No. I did." He shook it off for now. "It'll work out." He offered a hand. "See you next visit."

"Or sooner. I was serious about the kitten."

"Sure. They're going on five weeks now, so if you want to come sometime next week, you can see them."

"That would be great."

Will locked the door behind Todd. "Almost done, Tammie?"

"Just about." He could hear her doing stuff in the office space behind the wall, out of sight. She poked her head forward to the viewing window where he could see her. "If you want to head home, I'll only be a few more minutes."

"I can wait." He didn't like leaving the office separately, a holdover trait from working in busier locations. Jasper was probably as safe as Mayberry, but it didn't matter.

Once the office lights were out and doors were locked, they left for their parked cars. "See you in the morning, Tammie."

"'Night," she said, sliding behind the wheel to start the car.

Heaving a sigh, Will did the same. He was dreading facing those two kids after what he'd said. He and Parker knew what their intended plans were, but they'd said nothing to the kids. Neither wanted to get their hopes up only to have them crushed, or worse, if they didn't want to stay in Jasper with them. Realistically, their foster status *was* temporary. Whether the kids stayed until a more suitable home environment was found, or if they went the adoption route to keep Micah and Chelsea, fostering wasn't meant to be permanent. But he'd never intended to make them feel like they weren't wanted, that Will or even Parker were ready to let them go. Because they weren't. Not by a long shot.

Will turned up the AC in the car, then pulled from the parking area to the street. The kids had been living with them for not quite two months and he honestly couldn't imagine them not there now.

Everything in their lives now circled the kids, from the laundry to what they watched on TV. They'd jumped feet first into parenting. It wasn't a direction Will would have dreamed taking before Parker came into his life. He and Parker were also both hoping they were there to start school. Even though they shouldn't, they were making normal plans for the twins, like they were a family. Will's and Parker's family.

He frowned when he turned into the driveway to spot a truck he didn't know parked out front. That frown deepened when he discovered the truck had Texas plates.

Not good. He knew it wasn't Travis, and that didn't leave a lot of other people.

Unsure what to expect, he cautiously opened the front door. "I'm home," he called.

"Will!" screeched two joyful voices.

He sighed in a rush, grateful the incident at the dental office seemed to have been a forgotten fluke already.

"Hi there!" He knelt and scooped up a kid in each arm for hard hugs. He carefully looked at both, but saw no residual doubts leftover from his slip-up. He hugged them again in relief. "How's Tinker?"

"She's healthy!" Micah supplied. "Doctor Evans said she was a pretty cat."

Will smiled, then looked up when he heard cowboy boots on the wood floor. "Hi cowboy."

Parker smiled, but it was restrained. "We have company."

Will nodded, gaining his feet. "I saw the truck." Couldn't miss the thing, in fact.

Parker walked up to Will and greeted him with a swift but gentle kiss. "It's Kyle," he said quietly.

"What? Why?"

"I don't know. I wanted to wait until the kids were busy to talk to him."

Will got the hint. "Okay. Let me change and I'll take them to the barn to make sure Tinker's resting."

"Thanks." The shining light of love in his eyes melted Will.

"Come on, you two." Parker smiled at the twins. "Let's go finish your snack while Will changes, then you can show Will Tinker and the kittens."

They raced back to the dining table, both men watching them go. "Go do what you have to do," Will said.

"If something doesn't feel right, I just have to call Caleb to come kick his ass," Parker whispered, grinning with a hint of evilness.

"It's so good having the law in our family."

Parker chuckled. "Tell me about it. Go change. Whatever he wants can wait."

Will snatched another kiss before turning for their bedroom.

* * * *

Parker sauntered back to the kitchen. "Micah, keep it on your plate."

He hunted and found half his carrots had been pushed off the plate in his haste to put as much as possible into his mouth. Apparently carting a cat and family of kittens to the vet was hard work. He did notice Micah tended to avoid Kyle. Not that he blamed the boy. Parker wished he could avoid him, too.

Parker placed a mug of coffee on the table for Kyle.

"Thank you. I know this is—"

Parker shook his head. "It can wait."

Kyle shut his mouth, but nodded, sweetening the coffee instead. A few minutes later, Will appeared and Kyle stood from the table. He offered a hand. "I want to apologize for the way I was when you came to Texas."

Will glanced to Parker, who shrugged. He had no idea what Kyle's game was. Will accepted the offered hand. "Thank you."

"Okay, you two. Finish your snacks and juice then clean up. You can show Will Tinker while I talk to our guest."

Both kids stopped eating to look at Parker, Will, then shyly at Kyle, then drank down their juice. They put their dishes in the sink and went to wash up when they'd finished.

"They're a great pair of kids," Kyle offered once they were out of the room.

"They've come a long way since they've been here," Parker said. Micah was still shy of strangers, but to him, that really wasn't a bad trait to have.

Especially since he didn't trust the third man sitting at the table, himself.

"They're not Will's?" Kyle asked, searching between the two men with an air of surprise.

Parker hadn't realized it, but with Will's darker hair, he supposed they *could* be mistaken as his.

"No, we're fostering the twins." Will stood a little closer to Parker, a sign of solidarity.

"Better you than me," Kyle said without censure. "Not on my wish list, if you know what I mean."

"It's not for everyone," Parker agreed. "We love them to bits."

Kyle smiled kindly. "Then they're going to be just fine." He toasted both men with his coffee and took a sip.

The twins quickly rejoined them and Will led them away. "So what did Dr. Evans say about Tinker?"

Micah and Chelsea began to chatter simultaneously, their voices carrying through the house until they were outside. Parker wiped off the table and rinsed the dishes for the dishwasher before giving the man waiting his attention.

"All right, Kyle. Why are you here?" he asked, standing to the side. He leaned against the counter and crossed his arms and ankles.

Kyle swallowed, idly twisting his mug back and forth on the table before himself. "I wanted to say I was sorry," he started quietly. "I was a bastard to you and Will at your daddy's funeral."

"You drove all that way to apologize?" Parker snorted in sheer disbelief.

"Yes." Kyle looked up and for the first time, Parker saw the hollow emptiness of the man. "I loved him, for all the good it did me. He used me to hold the place together, then gave me a sinking ship."

"I don't care what kind of a relationship you had with my father." Frankly, Parker would rather not think about that at all. "What is wrong with the ranch?"

His suspicions were proven correct when Kyle said, "He's over a hundred grand behind in taxes. I don't know what he thought he was doing. He could have been paying, but when he fired Dawson, he dropped the ball on a lot of shit." Kyle stared at the coffee, a beaten man. "I never thought to ask because it wasn't what he hired me for."

"So what do you want from me?"

"Show me how he ran it all. I know the breeding, and the harvest schedule for the hay fields, but the money? I'm lucky to balance my own checkbook most weeks." He sighed, his shoulders slumped under the weight of it all. "Travis still won't do business with me, either. I'm losing money right and left and I can't find a way to stop it."

Parker let out a breath and tugged a chair from the table to sit on. "Have you tried talking to him? Like this?"

Kyle cursed quietly. "I had to drive to you. What do you think?"

"Have you talked to Dawson?"

Kyle nodded. "I guess you haven't heard yet. He's getting married this fall. The old coot found a woman." Kyle grinned some. "He's got a good one, though. Because of that, and her, he doesn't have the time to split between my spread and the Hopeck ranch. Can't blame him. She's a looker."

Parker rubbed his chin. No, he hadn't heard, but he hadn't talked much to Travis with him on the road again. He wondered how he and Eddie were doing. Something to do another day.

"How long would you need me there?"

Kyle perked up cautiously. "A few days? You understood your dad's methods, or at least would recognize his madness if you saw it."

Parker coughed into a fist, hiding most of his opinion. "That's one way of putting it." He stared at his dad's old foreman. "Give me one good reason why I should help you after what he, and you did?" He was far from convinced. That ranch was the black hole of everything bad that had happened in his life.

Kyle didn't blink. Parker wasn't even sure he was breathing. Then slowly, he came back to life.

"Honestly?" Parker scowled at him. "Right." Kyle adjusted on the kitchen chair. "I guess I deserved that," he mumbled. He framed his coffee mug between two work-roughened hands. "I want to get the ranch up to earning a profit again," he said. "I know it's a purely selfish thing, but that is home. I'd hate to see it sold for taxes when I know the money is there, waiting to be made." Kyle looked up. "I know it was your home, too. You're the one he shoulda given it to, no matter how he felt about— " His jaw snapped shut.

"Jesus, Kyle. You're gay and you can't even say it." He growled in disgust.

He sighed a rough rumble. "I know." He studied his coffee again. "If you help me save the ranch, I'll give you a percentage of the profits once the taxes are paid up. It's what he shoulda done to begin with, put it in holding for you until you were legal. I never wanted it, not if it took it away from you."

"Could've fooled me." Parker easily remembered his overjoyed cheering when Kyle learned he'd been willed the ranch instead of Chet's own son.

"I thought..." He scrubbed a hand over his face, pain shadowing a lot of the thoughts he couldn't hide. "What I thought really doesn't matter. I know the truth now." Kyle sought Parker from beneath lowered eyelids. "I mean it. You help me straighten out his mess, and I'll make you a legal shareholder of the property."

Parker leaned on his elbows, his hands clasped together on the table. He *really* wanted to tell the man no, but Kyle had come to him, had put aside his pride and his prejudices to sincerely ask, not just make a phone call to whine about his problems.

After a few tense, silent moments, he stated, "I can't make a decision like this without talking to Will first. I also have to think of the twins. They come first, always."

Kyle nodded, accepting if morose. "I understand. At least you didn't say no right off the bat." He stood from the chair to dig out his wallet. He found a card and handed it over. "That's got my cell number on it. I'm staying overnight at the inn, but will drive back in the morning." Parker palmed the card, pushing the chair under the table when he stood beside Kyle. "I don't expect an answer right now, but the sooner..." Kyle tried to smile, only managing a grimace and a shrug. "I know it's not your home any longer, and you don't think of it as such, but it is mine."

"Let me talk to Will," Parker repeated. He wasn't making any promises before he could do that.

Kyle shook a hand and with a nod, left. Parker shut the door behind him, resting with his spine against wood.

Why wouldn't that damn ranch just let him go?

Chapter Ten

Parker found Will and the kids in Tinker's stall in the barn. All three were sitting in loose hay, playing with the fuzzy monsters. They were a friendly bunch, at least. It would make them easy to rehome. He leaned over the top rail to watch, smiling and feeling a happiness that had been so very rare before landing in Jasper. Giggles and male laughter filled the barn. It was music.

Parker would never argue that Tinker had probably woven some sort of magic to help the twins feel at home. They'd all come from somewhere *out there*, to live with Will and Parker. Tinker was young, according to the vet, so she had won the lottery of a lifetime of good food and a whole barn at her disposal for a home. Parker had never been keen on housecats, but barn cats were free, and sometimes excellent, rodent control.

He rested his chin on folded arms, taking in the playing trio. Will spotted him first, glancing over a shoulder with a smile on his lips.

"How are the kittens?"

"Happy to be home, would be a good guess," Will told him, scratching one behind its tiny head. "Tinker still seems a little out of sorts."

Parker didn't doubt it. No one *liked* getting shots.

"Will said she's cranky because the doctor stuck her with a needle." Chelsea was carefully cuddling another kitten to her chest. Both kids had been shown how to hold a kitten safely and to only hold them for a few minutes at a time so they didn't overheat. Poor mama kitty was acting a little aloof, watching the shenanigans of her babies safely from her corner.

"I bet Will is right. It won't last." They'd guessed Tinker at one point had been a regular family cat because she didn't act feral. She was actually pretty friendly with all four of them now. How she'd wound up in their barn would always remain a mystery, but she was part of their family now, too. Parker wanted to make their family a reality, badly.

If helping Kyle jeopardized any part of Will's and Parker's future, especially with the twins, the answer would be a big, fat no.

* * * *

"I can't believe I'm even considering it," Parker groused, balling his shirt up to pitch hard into the dirty clothes that night. "Who will watch the kids? Take care of the horses? Summer's lessons?" Heck, the kids were starting school in a bare few weeks. So much he still had to do.

He faced Will who was also getting ready for bed. Parker's boots hit the floor, followed by jeans and underwear that went into the hamper. "I can't just leave."

Done stripping too, Will neared and ran a finger down the center of Parker's chest. "First, we find out if it's possible to take them with us. Second, if they can, we get one of the boarders, Jerry's always been reliable to lend a hand, to come by and help feed. If they can't go, then I find someone who can sit with them while I'm at work and you're gone. Babysitters are allowed on the short-term for emergencies."

"Not an emergency though." Parker walked to the bathroom to turn on the shower. Will followed.

He was trying to get to the root of Parker's thinking, but got the feeling his man didn't understand it all himself, not yet. If Parker felt the need to help Kyle, he'd support that, the same if he said no way. Understanding his reasoning for which direction he'd take?

Not the easiest.

"Remember what the case worker said. Treat them like they *are* our family. We can't stop living or having a life while they're here." It wasn't reasonable to believe that life would be put on hold while they were fostering, to begin with. It wasn't always easy to find the happy medium, but they were trying. Will tucked up against Parker's back and looped tender arms around his waist while the water heated. "Why are you, by the way? You'd said no way when he'd called."

Kyle had been a royal dick to Will in the past. He wasn't thrilled that Parker was giving him the benefit of the doubt now. It was because Will was feeling protective of the children, though, and he knew that. If Parker felt this was something he should do, Parker could handle Kyle and any bullshit he brought with him.

"It takes a humble man to do what he did," Parker said solemnly. "I saw it in his eyes. My dad stole from him as much as he stole from me. Saddling him with the ranch was a punishment. My guess is Dad never thought to see me again, having made me dead in his mind. He found a sucker to bleed dry emotionally and then repaid that by ruining him financially."

"Geez," Will hissed. "Your dad was the devil on legs."

Parker's frame jerked when he snorted. "I'm glad he did what he did now. I can't imagine living with the man Kyle knew." Parker cupped over Will's clutched hands with his own. "I guess I feel sorry for him now, to be honest. Sixteen years under Dad's roof and four years of hell got me you and my outrageous family here. What did living through his hell get Kyle? A ranch that's days from crashing and burning, no friends, and no help. Dad had him hating himself so much, he finished ruining the ranch by being everything my dad made him believe he was. Something dirty," he whispered.

"Parker," Will said, swallowing to hide the deeper ache in his throat. "Okay, I understand now." If Kyle could turn the ranch around, then it would be like giving Chet the middle finger. It wouldn't fix everything, and certainly wouldn't heal Kyle, but it would be a start. "I guess the next question is do you want all of us to go?"

"Of course!" Parker tapped his hands for Will to let go and climbed into the shower, Will right behind him. He loved getting soapy and wet with his husband. It usually led to other naked activities.

Once situated, Will said, "Okay. I'll call the case worker in the morning to see what our options are. If it's a go, I'll leave the rest up to you." Personally, he'd rather not deal with Kyle. Bureaucracy he could handle.

Parker spun, making water splash off his shoulders, to embrace Will. "Thank you."

"In this together," Will murmured. Body heat, more than the steamy water, was beginning to muddle his thoughts. Staring into Parker's eyes, his breathing hitched. He hoped the wanting he found there never faded. "Let's get clean. Haven't been able to touch you in too long."

Parker groaned right when Will ghosted over his lips. A full body shiver stole over the man in his arms.

"Soap. Clean," Will pressed when Parker tried to lengthen the kiss. Tonight, he was going to make his man fly.

Parker relinquished his hold to face the wall. Gathering the sponge and dousing it with water then soap, he handed it over a shoulder then spread himself for Will's exploration.

Will cupped a butt cheek and squeezed, getting a throaty moan in reply. He took his time scrubbing over Parker's shoulders, massaging as he washed. He watched Parker's head slowly sag, relaxing beneath the heat of the shower and Will's hands. Parker worked hard, feared no physical labor, and the pride he took in his work was evident in the care of the horses and the upkeep of the barn and house. Stroking over hardened muscles while cleaning all that wonderful skin was a pleasure for both of them.

Turning him around, Will took his time finishing his task, taking care around Parker's balls and further. He was already planning what he was going to do once they were in bed. Glancing up, he snagged on half-closed eyes, Parker panting quietly.

"I love that grin you get," Parker said, his voice husky. "The Doctor Evil with a plan grin. Love it."

Will smirked. "Too easy to guess what I'm planning, huh?"

"Makes me harder just thinking about it."

"Like making you feel that good," Will admitted. He stroked Parker's length in punctuation, watching as his eyes completely drifted shut and his lips parted with a slow exhale. Parker may be able to tell what was lurking behind Will's grin, but there was no hiding the pleasure on Parker's face.

Cupping water over his chest, Will roamed with attentive hands, rinsing away the last of the soap bubbles. He then leaned close and licked over a nipple while slowly stroking Parker's cock in his hand. He moved across his chest to do the same to the other side. Parker trembled.

He hated to let go, but they had to get out of the shower eventually if he wanted to do more, and Will wanted a *lot* more. "Go dry off, sweetheart. I'll be right there."

Parker's eyes lazily blinked open. Water drops clung to his lashes. He moved like he was entranced, stiffly if carefully slipping out of the tub to swipe a towel over himself and his hair. Will dove under the water stream and washed up, clean and turning off the water before Parker had even made it out of the bathroom.

Will trailed him across the bedroom, wanting to devour every inch of Parker, taste him, and hear the moans that his man made when he was utterly shattered with pleasure.

Following Parker onto the bed, he pushed him over to his back, to slink up his naked body until he could find Parker's lips for a heady kiss. Parker hummed, widening his legs for Will to blanket him. Skin brushed skin. Firm but gentle fingers dug into Will's hair. Slow passion simmered, unhurried. Will took his time, adoring Parker with his fingers and lips, tasting and teasing with his tongue. Parker mewled and moaned between rasped gasps of breath.

He swirled his tongue over Parker, loving the way his dick twitched, as though seeking more, reaching for Will.

When he swept lower, Parker's groan lengthened, deepened, creating goose bumps up and down Will's spine. He smiled, but didn't slow down.

"Will." Parker stretched out hunting fingers but Will was beyond his reach.

Will ignored him. Well, his pleas, not him. He shifted on the bed, finding one of those spots that he'd learned melted Parker like butter in a fire.

"Fuck," he whimpered when Will's tongue found its target.

Will doubled his attention and soon Parker was trembling beneath his lips. Skin flushed with need and desire quivered with every fresh stroke. Hefting up the length of Parker's shaft, he dragged his tongue, slowly tantalizing every inch all the way to the swollen, damp tip. He licked his lips before capturing Parker in his mouth to suck— hard.

"Will!" He grabbed a pillow to bite, shaking his head roughly on the bed. Will chuckled quietly, giving him a few seconds to catch his breath.

Reaching for the lube he'd stashed on the bed before their shower, he eased into Parker's entrance, distracting him by whipping his tongue against the sensitive points of his cock. Parker was mumbling incoherently.

Will moved closer while Parker hefted his legs.

"Please," he whined, watching Will with a heat in his gaze that could have set the room on fire.

Will braced himself, filling Parker slowly, lovingly. He loved everything about Parker. *Making love* was the pinnacle of being able to show him how much, how deeply he felt it all. There weren't many reasons Parker was like this: open, vulnerable. In their bedroom, he gave himself over to Will unselfishly. Will always wanted to let him know, to *feel* what that meant to him. Each beat of his heart was echoed by the deep stroke and heat of Parker's body holding his.

Parker flexed and Will's eyes crossed. He moaned, losing his concentration. "Parker."

Will shifted on the bed, urging Parker. His thrusts grew more determined, deeper, and he swore he saw heaven in Parker's blazing gaze. Parker raised a hand to stroke himself. Lightning struck with the contact. Watching him, Will's mind simply unplugged, his body taking over while synapses popped and sizzles burst under heated skin.

Then Parker was groaning, his body tightening and Will couldn't hold it any longer. Sweat dampened his brow as it all crashed around him. Tension rolled down his frame as he jetted into Parker's body. Liquid heat.

"Oh, God." Parker's eyes slammed shut and he twitched on the bed, unloading onto his chest in thick, white spurts.

Flushed skin, glazed eyes, and a supple mouth were Will's view as Parker slowly rolled his hand over his length, prolonging the enjoyment. There was a last clench and Will's body collapsed on top of Parker, just...boneless.

Both panted, breathless and limp. Parker's captured hand wiggled out from between them to loop over Will's shoulders. Twisting his head on the pillow, he pressed soft lips to Will's temple. "Love you."

Will nodded, still trying to catch his breath. "Going to be the death of me. That was..."

"Uh huh," Parker agreed groggily. "Wow."

Will chuckled roughly then made himself fall to the side, letting Parker breathe more easily.

"Love you, too," Will said.

Fingers stroked his back. They needed to clean up, but... Moving was overrated.

Chapter Eleven

Will hung up the phone at his desk with a severely trembling hand. Parker's heart was going to be crushed. The conversation he'd just had was supposed to end in a completely different way.

Instead, Will was close to tears.

He covered his face with splayed palms. "This is going to destroy him," he choked out. He tried to even his breathing, but wasn't doing a great job of it.

"Well, what did they say?" Tammie asked from the doorway.

Will shook his head.

"Oh, that sucks. I know you and Parker really wanted to— "

"They have an adoption petition open on the twins," he choked out.

She gasped. "What?"

"The last home visit they did. They didn't even tell us it was possible. They were evaluated for adoption and cleared."

Tammie stumbled forward to almost fall into Will's spare chair in front of his desk. "No," she whispered in horror.

He scrubbed over his eyes and looked up to nod. "I beat their phone call by a few hours." He snorted mockingly. "They want to set up a meeting time with the potential couple this weekend."

Tears rolled down Tammie's face. "That's not fair! You should have been first choice."

Will growled. Clearly they weren't. They'd been biding their time to do their own petition, wanting to have as strong a case as possible so there'd be no denial.

"Why didn't they put you two first?" Tammie reached for a tissue off his desk and blew her nose.

Will shrugged, though he was pretty sure he could take a damn good stab at the answer. *Same-sex couple.* Swinging between heartbroken himself and worried about Parker, he was furious at the injustice of the whole system.

"What am I going to tell him?" Will wondered, wiping over watery eyes.

Tammie shook her head, her eyes glistening with more tears. "I don't know. Those kids are his world."

The dental office front door opened, turning Tammie in her seat. "I'll give you a few minutes," she said, then stood to greet Will's patient.

He appreciated her thoughtfulness, but the future was already set. Somehow he had to find a way to tell Parker that wouldn't destroy him. He couldn't begin to think of what the kids would think, if they'd feel betrayed. As their fosters, Will and Parker had never made overtures that this *couldn't* happen. They'd done their best to give them the support and safety that both Micah and Chelsea had needed, that would never change, whether they stayed or left.

So what makes these people so much better than we have already proven we could be? What can they do that we haven't? Why didn't they say something when they came to the house last time? There'd been zero hint that outside adoption was part of the evaluation. They'd talked to both kids, saw how happy they were, how well-adjusted.

He wanted to call Melody, or even Ms. Ross to see what had happened. When was the petition for the kids opened? Why weren't they told?

Unfortunately, it was a phone call he couldn't make right that second with a patient waiting.

He wiped his face one last time, putting it to the back of his mind. Will wished the rest of it would be that easy to ignore.

* * * *

Getting home that evening, loud squeals and laughter floated from the backyard when he got out of the car.

His heart still ached because he'd found no magic message in a bottle to break that afternoon's news to Parker.

Walking through the house to the rear, he opened the door to find both kids running around like crazy, dashing through a water sprinkler. Parker had Tank tied to one of the tether poles, brushing him down within easy eyeball view of the twins. It looked like he'd given the horse a bath, too.

Will stood to the side and simply watched them. Carefree and happy. He wanted to remember this in case things moved quickly for the twins from there.

Parker stopped what he was doing when he noticed Will was home. He circled the wet ground and stopped at Will's shoulder. "What's wrong?"

Will shook his head, bottling it up for now. He guessed he hadn't been doing a good job of hiding his thoughts again.

He'd gotten more information during the last phone call. It made more sense, but it wasn't going to be any easier to explain. It had all sounded very dismissive to him. Superficial explanations. He swallowed the sigh. "I'll tell you later." When Parker looked at him with a huge frown on his face, Will added, "I promise."

Will faced the kids. "Okay you two! Let's rinse off and go shower inside. I feel like burgers!"

Dual cheers were shouted loud and clear. Parker turned down the water to unhook the sprinkler, then made sure each kid got a good rinse. "Grab a towel," he called before they could charge inside, sopping wet.

Parker turned off the water and rolled up the hose. "Let me put Tank in the pasture."

Will nodded. "I'll be inside." He didn't want to let the twins have too much time to become distracted from their mission of getting clean and dry.

Parker gave him another questioning head tilt, but when Will couldn't find the words, he turned away to lead Tank to join the other horses. Will shut the house door behind him, clearing the living room to check on the kids.

"Bath time!" he called.

The sound of bare feet scampering across the floor made his heart ache. He did not want to let them go. Selfishly, he hoped something didn't connect. Either they hated the kids on sight, or the kids were terrified of them. It wasn't fair to want either to happen, and he knew that.

Foster was temporary. They'd both known that going in. Except they'd both thought there would be a chance... Will walked into the bathroom to start the water, trying to not dwell on it. He didn't want to worry the kids with his moods. Micah had beat him into the bathroom, already getting the tub ready, tossing in a few toys.

"Just a couple for tonight. Your sister needs to clean up too."

"She can play with this one!" He held up one of his floating trains.

"I'm sure she'll appreciate it. Okay, into the water." He swirled it to even out the heat. Micah clambered over the edge and plopped into the water. Getting down on his knees, Will shampooed his hair, listening as Micah made sputtering noises with the trains he'd chosen. "How about a haircut before dinner?" He tugged gently on the locks that had grown out.

Micah didn't so much as twitch at the suggestion. The youngster had really come out of his shell in the last weeks. Summer was their best friend. Sunday breakfast was like a party. They were even excited, if cautious, about school.

He really hoped the couple they were going to meet knew what they were getting in these two kids.

With Micah sparkly, Chelsea was next, in and out of the tub, clean and dashing to her room to find clothes. Will rinsed out the tub for a second time, putting away the kids' toys in the small basket for them.

"Hey, you going to change?" Parker asked with laughing concern from the doorway.

Will looked at himself. "Yeah, I guess I should." He was still in his work scrubs. He stood and faced the man watching him.

Parker tipped his chin, his gaze missing nothing. He moved a few inches out of the way when Will got closer to let him pass.

"What is wrong?" Parker asked with a little more directness.

Will looked down the hall, checking for the kids, but only heard them in their rooms. His feet almost dragged when he headed for the bedroom. He was dreading breaking this to Parker.

With his husband on his heels, Will entered the bedroom. Parker closed the door and sat on the bed.

"I called to see about taking them with us," he said, not even sure where to start.

Parker sighed, his shoulders slumping. "They said no, didn't they?"

Will sat beside his hip. "Worse. There's a couple looking to adopt them. They're setting up a meeting time for this weekend."

"What!" Parker's head snapped up and he shook hard, his eyes blooming wide in pain. "No!" He shot to his feet, marching to the door. Only...he stopped and sagged into it. "No," he whimpered.

Will walked up behind him and cradled him between his arms, resting his head to Parker's back. "They're not gone," he said. "Just want to meet."

Parker shuddered. Will felt his pain acutely.

"We never had a chance, did we?"

Will trembled, blinking to block the tears he felt pressing hard. "I have to think we did, and maybe... Maybe we still do." He released a shaky, pent-up breath.

"Just not with Chelsea and Micah." Parker slumped. "I love them, Will."

Will petted his stomach, nuzzling from behind. "I do too."

Parker turned in his arms, gripping him in a trembling embrace. "They have to come first, but fuck, I didn't realize it would hurt to have to let them go. Not like this."

"I know, sweetheart. I didn't either."

The rushed clomp of two pairs of feet stampeded past their door, forcing the men apart.

"Better change," Will mumbled. Parker nodded without energy.

"At least now I know why you suggested burgers."

"Yeah. Lucy's is exactly what we need."

Parker snorted softly. He tilted for a kiss. "They'll be okay, and so will we."

Will knew he was saying that to sound like he was at peace with the decision. Will knew better. Parker's heart was breaking, the same as his own was.

After changing, they loaded up into the car and drove the short distance to the center of Jasper.

Will motioned down the block to the front door of Lucy's. "Go get a table. Shouldn't take too long to get him a trim."

Parker nodded, his eyes heavy with sadness.

Will held Micah's hand and walked down the sidewalk to the barber. One of the few he'd seen that still had the actual spinning, striped barber poles outside on the wall. *Another era going extinct.*

The small cowbell jingled when he opened the door. The four chair shop wasn't busy at that time of the day. Two huge mirrors covered opposing walls. Will imagined it was a pretty hopping place on the weekends.

"Evening," the lone barber called.

"Got time for one more?" he asked, shaking Micah's little hand to show who he meant.

"For little man? Of course!" He smiled and waved him over. He spun the chair, letting him climb up on the seat.

Micah smiled when the barber swung out the cape with a *whoosh* sound. A quick question or two, and within minutes, Micah's mop was gone, leaving a cute, smiling face. *Got to make him look good for tomorrow*. And Will hated that reason.

"So you guys headed home?"

"Nope!" Micah piped up. "Goin' to Lucy's for burgers!"

The barber chuckled, flipping the body cape away. "Well, you two have a nice dinner."

Will paid him and with a smaller hand in his, turned to guide him from the shop. Micah skipped at his side down the sidewalk, singing his ABCs. Will sighed, listening to every single sound.

These were the moments he was going to miss the most.

Chapter Twelve

Parker fought to not clutch Chelsea's hand, while Will held Micah's as all four strolled the downtown sidewalks Saturday. Parker was trying to keep the worst of the turmoil snaking through his gut off his face. Mr. Jacks, the children's advocacy lawyer, had called that morning to confirm the time and place.

There weren't many places conducive to a casual meeting, so they were going to Lucy's again. They were a few minutes early. Considering the energy the twins had that morning, being early at all was a little bit of a miracle.

"Hi guys!" Lucy called from the counter, all smiles to see them when they walked through the door.

"Hi Lucy." Will caught Parker's glance. "We're meeting some people so can we have the back room?" he told her.

"Sure. How many?"

"Three more," Will answered. "We just need quiet for a little while. Business."

Lucy took a longer look at all of them, then nodded. "Sure," she said gentler. "I'll let them know when they get here where you are."

Parker followed Will as they slipped between tables and booths until they reached the private party room. "How will she know?" Parker whispered over Will's shoulder.

"I don't think it's going to be hard to pick out three strangers in their Sunday best on a Saturday," he replied lowly.

Parker looked at the kids, and then themselves. And sighed. He had a point. Chelsea wore a cute pale yellow and blue summer dress and sandals, and Micah was in jeans and a shirt. The kids were practically sparkling, they were so neat and clean. Parker wasn't overdressed, he rarely wore more than jeans, but Will was in slacks and a nice pullover. Chelsea's hair was in a clipped tail, and with Micah's new hair trim, they all looked too put together for just lunch out. A marked difference from dinner the night before.

"I'll bring the kids some juice until the others get here," Lucy said, leaving them in the room to get settled at a large table.

"Thanks." Parker pulled out a chair for Chelsea.

She was being unusually subdued. Parker guessed it was too much to hope their internal fears weren't being picked up by the twins. Both Parker and Will were anxious about this meeting. They'd had so little time to mentally prepare, neither had said a word to the children about what this was about. What could they tell them? The energy the kids had left the house with for coming to Lucy's two days in a row seemed to have dwindled considerably with that uncertainty hounding them both.

Parker released a slow breath, trying to dispel the worst of his fears. He had to think of the twins' happiness and safety first. It wasn't easy because he knew they were perfectly safe and happy with him and Will. He only wished everyone else would see that and leave them alone.

Several minutes later, Lucy reappeared carrying two covered cups, followed by Mr. Jacks and two more Parker didn't know. He stood from the table.

"Mr. Vandersoot. Mr. Parkinson." Mr. Jacks greeted both and shook their hands. "Hi kids," he offered calmly, if upbeat.

They quietly said hello without looking up. Parker wanted to bury them against his chest, take them far away from that room. They knew something was up, and he felt like a total sleaze for doing this to them.

Only...it wasn't his choice and it was out of his hands.

"Micah, Chelsea, please tell Mr. Jacks hello properly."

They each stood and shook his hand.

"Thank you, kids. You've grown so much since I saw you." He smiled. They didn't. It seemed seeing him again deflated them even more. It tore at Parker's heart. They knew Mr. Jacks meant changes. The couple that had followed Mr. Jacks into the room were in the background and they were waved forward. "Micah, Chelsea, this is David and Rita. They came a long way to meet you."

Graciously, if quietly, the kids offered a hand to say hello to the two strangers.

"Let's all sit for now," Will offered. Everyone took a chair. The two newcomers sat across from the kids.

"Thank you for letting us meet up on a Saturday," Rita said, smiling warmly. "You both look just like your photos." She took her time to study the kids across from her.

Their silence was deafening.

Parker looked at Rita across from him, and felt it in his stomach. She was smitten. But one look at

David's face and he knew he'd deck the bastard for saying one wrong word. His opinions were clear in his gaze.

Lucy came in and a little of the tension faded with the disruption. "If you want to order drinks, I'll be happy to, or if you want to wait..."

"Just a water for me," Mr. Jacks told her.

"Coffee, please," David said with a raw, nasal accent.

"Sweet tea for me, please," Rita added.

"The usual for you guys?" Lucy asked expectantly.

"Please," Will replied.

Parker nodded in agreement. Yeah, they'd been there often enough that Lucy knew them pretty well by this point. Parker and Will had been customers almost since they'd started dating.

Parker couldn't help himself with the constant judgmental staring coming from the other side of the table. He put an arm around Chelsea protectively. She burrowed into his side, hiding. "They're shy with strangers. It's not personal," he said.

"That's to be expected. We know their background."

Parker almost snarled at David's imperious tone, like they had any part of what had happened to the twins *before*. Before they'd come to Jasper. Before with their mother. Before they'd found a taste of safety. Instead of jumping across the table, he buried his nose in Chelsea's hair. "It's going to be all right." She shivered.

The uncomfortable tension levels were quickly climbing through the roof. There was an instant dislike emanating from the children and whether Mr. Jacks was aware or not, Parker could see it as easily as his own fingers. The kids did not like David or Rita, and were terrified of the situation. Silence stretched.

Mr. Jacks cleared his throat, whatever he was about to say cutoff by David.

"Well, when do we get to talk to them alone?" he demanded, breaking the silence as skillfully as a bull in a china shop.

Will stiffened on the chair on Micah's opposite side. "When we all feel they're comfortable enough to do that," he answered with no less of a growl in his own voice. "These are two children, not pound puppies to be debated and handed over. Their opinions matter in this also. Their comfort is all I care about and right now, you're frightening them."

Micah twisted and climbed out of his seat to sit on Will's lap. Lucy reappeared then with a tray of drinks.

"Chelsea, Micah? Can we talk to you?" Rita asked gently. "I'd really like to get to know you both."

She poked out from where she hid, full of suspicion. "Why? Mr. Jacks? Are you going to take us away again? I don't want to go! You said we'd be safe here!" She started to cry.

Parker rocked her, trying to soothe her. "You are safe, baby. Always."

"I told you." David stood from his chair with a jarring jolt, almost knocking into Lucy and a braced tray of drinks. "You can't trust people like them to not screw with their heads."

Parker's eyes bulged. "What's that supposed to mean?"

"Does your condition make you an idiot as well as a deviant?" he hissed scornfully.

"Now wait just a minute," Will interjected, curling Micah into his chest.

"David, you were told who the fosters were—" Mr. Jacks stood as well. Displeasure and anger had taken the place of the unbiased mediator.

"And look what they've done to these two!" He waved a hand in Parker's direction, sneering with distaste. Obviously Chelsea standing up for herself and demanding answers was not something David approved of.

"All they've done is shown them love and support," a woman said from the doorway. Parker dipped his head. This was going to hell in a fast hurry.

"This is a private meeting," David snapped.

"Not when you attack one of this town's residents." Jeannie walked in with nearly a dozen people on her heels. "How dare you come here and put down the best people these two children have in their lives?"

Will gulped, his eyes bugging out also. "Jeannie, please. Not helping."

"Bull phooey." She glared at David, saying, "Chelsea, baby. Summer is at the counter with Aunt Wanda having a piece of Lucy's chocolate pie. Take your brother out to them, okay?"

When Chelsea swept upward to look at Parker, he nodded. "Go," he whispered. "We'll be right there to go home. I promise." He kissed Chelsea on the forehead. "Micah, go with Sissy."

He slid from Will's lap and both practically ran from the room. He wished he could escape with them.

Instead, Parker stood, glad to be able to say what he'd been holding on his tongue.

"I don't give a rat's ass what you think of me, but never *and I mean never* speak to me or my family like that again. Those kids are still healing. They're scared. They knew as soon as we got here something was up. They're not dumb and I can guarantee you will never get to "talk" to those two alone. Ever."

"Parker!" Will gasped.

Parker turned to Mr. Jacks. "Thank you for bringing them, now please make sure they leave town."

"They're not your family," David jeered with sheer revulsion.

Mr. Jacks seemed taken aback by the crudeness of his insult. He was shaking his head, muttering apologies to Will.

Parker's lip twitched into a near snarl. "This town is my family," he warned. And David was about three seconds from meeting a lot of them from the ground, looking up.

A hand on his arm stopped him from circling the table. Will's grip was relentless.

"Only because we haven't started the paperwork ourselves."

There. It had been said. All eyes turned to Will.

Mr. Jacks gathered his briefcase, scowling at David. He said to Will, "I'll let my superiors know that is your wish. How do the kids feel about staying?"

"We haven't asked them yet," Will said. "This meeting was just sprung on us yesterday."

Mr. Jacks frowned. "It shouldn't have been." He put his case back down. "Let me walk David and Rita out. I'll be back."

Jeannie neared, standing in solidarity. Considering she was so much shorter than everyone, it was really kind of cute.

"I'm sorry," Will told Rita. "I hope you find what you're looking for."

Rita studied the room of people. "It's pretty clear they have an incredible support group behind them."

She shook her head sadly. "I couldn't take them from that. They have a family here."

"An accidental family," Will agreed. "We've never told them about our plans for the future. We never once told them this couldn't happen either."

Parker knew the only guarantee they had was their mother could never find them, and if by some fluke she did, then they could protect the twins by getting the law involved. If they wanted to find her when they were of age, they had the right, but he prayed like a penitent pastor that they never felt that desire to reconnect.

"That's good to know." Mr. Jacks directed the visiting couple to the door. "I'll be right back."

Once Mr. Jacks and the other two left the room, Will demanded, "Okay, how many of you did Lucy call?"

Abashed, Jeannie and four more held up their hands. Will covered his face with a palm, shook his head and then started to laugh. A few smiled in commiseration and humor, but none in the room looked even a smidge shamefaced. "You know, I'm going to have to tell him, right?"

"Actually, Tammie called me last night," Jeannie admitted. "I already knew they were coming. Lucy just let me know they'd arrived. Heck, we're only a couple of doors down. Of course we'd be here for you. I had no idea what they'd be like, but when I heard him... He's lucky I didn't come in here and kick his ass for you."

Parker and Will both smiled. "You got to love a small town grapevine."

"It works," she said without guilt, rolling a shoulder. "No one is going to hurt those babies."

"I'm glad to hear that."

Jeannie gasped and whirled. Mr. Jacks stood in the doorway.

"Well, it's the truth." She staunchly crossed her arms over her chest.

He waved a hand to calm her down, entering the room. "Let's talk for a few minutes." He retook his chair.

Will kissed her on the cheek. "Go with the cavalry. Keep an eye on the twins. We'll be out in a few minutes." She stared at Mr. Jacks suspiciously. "Really," he emphasized.

When she left, everyone who'd been hanging around left with her.

"I'm so sorry about that," Will started. He quickly explained what had happened, making Mr. Jacks laugh.

"I will admit that kind of interference wouldn't go over with a lot of case workers, but it's good to know so many here really do care about them." He brought up his briefcase, opening it. "So they really only told you yesterday about today's introduction?"

"Yes. I was told there was an open file on the twins, and in the same breath, they wanted to make this meeting."

Mr. Jacks blinked a few times. "Well, that's a definite drop of the info ball. Sorry about that. Now what was this about wanting to start paperwork?"

Parker and Will shared a look. Will reached for his hand under the table and Parker scooted a little closer on his chair. "We were going to wait a couple of months, but if the twins are happy, and want to stay, we want to keep them here. As ours."

"This didn't influence your decision?"

Will shook his head. "No. We knew by the second week they were here. They fit." He squeezed Parker's hand. "But we knew we weren't an ideal choice because we're gay."

Mr. Jacks cupped his hands on the table. "Gentlemen, I can tell you up front that can't and won't have a bearing on any decision the state court makes."

"Then why weren't we more informed? Why did they try to adopt them without at least giving us a chance?" Parker asked abruptly.

"An educated guess? Simply because they haven't been with you that long. You don't have a recorded history, and they're your first fosters. Some only manage one contract, or decide they don't want to uphold even that one anymore and send the kids back into the system. It's a case of needing to make sure you both were capable, and that they were settled, I'm sure."

Parker shook his head, almost ill hearing that. He swallowed down the bitterness. The thought of simply returning kids... It went against everything he himself believed in, especially considering his own history. "We did this knowing it could be short or long-term, but we've wanted to adopt since before we were married."

"We love those two, and we both think they feel the same way," Will added solemnly.

"Why don't we ask them?" he offered with open palms.

"Is that a good idea after...?" Will motioned to the untouched drinks at the now empty seats.

"They'll be asked more than once over the course of the filing and hearing dates how they feel about becoming a family." He smiled encouragingly. "Though from what I saw here today, I sincerely doubt you'll have any issues. It's pretty clear they've grown to trust you both, as well as the people they're familiar with here. I wouldn't want to force them into a new environment if you're both serious about wanting to proceed."

Parker knew he was, and by Will's expression, there would be no stopping him.

Will drew a breath and faced Parker. "Ready to be dads?"

"I think we already are," he said, grinning. Will chuckled then released him.

He left to gather the kids to see if they were right in what they believed the kids wanted.

Chapter Thirteen

The diner's main room had filled up since they'd arrived for their meeting. Will hid his chuckle, wondering exactly how many were there for the kids and how many were there for Saturday lunch. There were a few curious stares, and a few smiles, but after David and Rita's departure, it didn't appear that anything more was going to happen.

Will put a light hand on Chelsea's shoulder. "Hey, you two ready for some lunch?" They'd been making good headway on a piece of chocolate pie with Summer, but he wasn't going to give them or Wanda a hard time about it. Nothing could distract like Lucy's pie. He smiled for them. "The mean couple is gone. It's just us and Mr. Jacks, and you both like Mr. Jacks, remember? He brought you to us."

Chelsea shared a look with her brother then slowly nodded. She put down her fork. "Are we in trouble again?"

Will bent to pluck her off the stool she sat on to gather her in his arms. "No, baby. In fact, this might be the best day for all of us. But you have to come see why."

She blinked big brown eyes at him, full of wary disbelief. Will's heart ached.

He dropped a hand for Micah. Hesitantly, he took the offered hand and slid off his stool seat.

"You're not in trouble. On Lucy's pie, I wouldn't lie about that."

"What does that mean?" she asked.

He took a slow step, to keep both listening. "If I'm wrong, you can eat all the pie you want, but if I'm not lying and it's going to be okay, then you both eat lunch with us like we always do, together. Deal?"

Micah stared at him hard. "We're not in trouble?"

"Nope."

"Can I go too?" Summer asked, ready to hop off her padded stool and join them. Will paused as Wanda answered.

"Why don't we let them have their lunch first and then we'll see, okay?"

She pouted but didn't seem overly upset by the decision. "Then we'll play."

Chelsea wanted to nod, Will could see it, but she was terrified all over again. He kissed her cheek. He'd give anything to give them back the security they'd awakened with that morning.

Leading Micah by the hand, he walked past Jeannie to carry Chelsea into the room and let the kids have their original seats, between him and Parker. Will noticed someone had come in and taken away the untouched drinks.

Mr. Jacks was writing on a legal pad at his elbow. "I'll confer with my notes at the office and set a court date with the judge, provided..." He smiled at the kids. "Chelsea. Micah. Are you happy in Jasper?"

Will stroked Micah's hair. When Micah clammed up, he told him, "It's okay. Nothing bad is going to happen. This is just like when Lois comes to the house to see how you're doing."

Slowly, the kids nodded.

"Do you like Will and Parker? They treat you nice?"

Chelsea nodded, then said, "He's teaching us to ride horses."

Parker flushed. "Well, teaching them care and safety. They haven't been on one yet."

Mr. Jacks chuckled warmly. "That sounds like fun. Would it make you happy to stay here? Forever?"

Two sets of eyes stared, wide and unsure. "Forever?" Chelsea whispered.

"If you want," Parker said softly to both of them. "Will and I would like to be your dads. Your forever and ever dads."

"No more leaving?" Micah asked shakily.

"Never ever again," Will stressed. "You'd live with us, as a family."

"And with Tinker?" Micah asked.

Will grinned, lighthearted. "Yes, and with Tinker." At Mr. Jacks questioning expression, he clarified, "We had a barn cat adopt us and give us kittens."

"We help take care of her," Micah offered without being prodded.

"You do?"

Both Chelsea and Micah nodded firmly.

"So if you never had to leave Tinker, Will, or Parker, would that be okay with the both of you?" he asked.

"What about Mom?" Chelsea asked. She scooted close to Parker. He wrapped an arm over her shoulders, tucking her into his side.

"You're safe," Mr. Jacks replied. "She can't find you and she's not supposed to try, either."

Will knew the woman was in jail and wouldn't be out for several years, but it broke his heart knowing the twins still lived with the fear that she'd return and hurt them more. It would take a long time to get rid of those demons.

"We're asking you both, because you both matter to us," Will said. "Do you want to stay with us, but not as fosters or as guardians. We want to be your dads, permanently and forever. Will you let us?" He'd give anything to not have any more Davids or Ritas show up on their doorstep. First he wanted to keep them safe. Hopefully that led to keeping them happy.

"Can I call you Dad?" Micah wondered. "I've never had a dad."

Will swallowed thickly. "If you want to. I'd love that."

"Parker can be Pop," Chelsea chimed in. "Is that okay?" Big brown eyes peered upward at him from where she sat next to him, swinging from one man to the other, waiting for their verdict.

Parker's eyes were glistening. "I think that's perfectly okay."

"Wonderful," Mr. Jacks said, smiling brightly. "Give me a few days to get with the judge and I'll see about scheduling a hearing."

Micah reached up and tugged on Will's shirt sleeve. "Can we have pie now?"

All three men chuckled. "Let's have lunch, then we'll see about pie, how's that?" Will suggested. He reached a hand across chairs and grazed the back of Parker's neck, sharing the knowledge and happiness of what they'd just put into motion. "Going to be a family."

"And we have an amazing family," Parker agreed.

Without warning, a huge cheer erupted in the main dining hall. Will jerked and Parker's gaze widened.

"What the...?" Parker muttered. He stood from the table and walked to the doorway. Once there, the cheering intensified and he started to laugh until he was holding his middle, almost bent double.

"You're never going to believe this!" he shouted over his shoulder.

The group in the private room stood and crowded around the double-wide doorway to see just what was going on.

Someone had hurriedly hung a *Congratulations!* banner above the eatery counter. And every single person in the place was standing, cheering, and applauding.

"I guess that means a formal announcement isn't necessary," Mr. Jacks joked, clapping both Will and Parker lightly on the shoulder. Micah and Chelsea were staring, gaping from between legs to the celebrating going on before them.

Will got a tug on his shoulder and he inched away from the slowly calming crowd.

"I don't want to put a damper on this, but it's not done yet. The judge has the final approval."

Will understood the warning, didn't like it, but he understood. "Do you believe for an instant he'd refuse these kids an entire town for a family?"

Mr. Jacks let out a slow breath. "Honestly, not in the least. But I have to let you know that."

"I know. But we didn't get this far by thinking tomorrow would never happen."

"We better see about lunch," Parker warned over a shoulder.

"Why?" Will asked seeing the playfulness behind his broad grin.

"Lucy just offered pie to everyone. On the house!"

"Pie! Pie!" The kids cheered, starting to jump up and down. The disaster of the previous meeting was quickly—thankfully—becoming a fading memory for them.

"I guess we're having pie for lunch," Will said. He saw no reason to fight a losing battle. They could have lunch later, or tomorrow.

* * * *

Will glanced toward the passed out kids in the backseat via the rearview mirror. Word had quickly gotten out that they'd started the process to adopt the twins. It was probably the busiest Lucy's had been since she'd opened.

Jeannie had been standing right outside the room when they'd started to discuss the matter with Mr. Jacks, managing to overhear enough. When they started to ask the children how they felt about it all, she'd issued quick orders. In about five minutes flat, she'd commandeered the restaurant and anyone within reach to do her bidding.

And Will thought Wanda was the powerhouse of the baking duo.

Jeannie proved him wrong. Wanda was just the saner of the two. Jeannie was clearly the more mischievous. She'd been able to pull together a party in minutes.

Before too long, most of Parker's family had arrived at the diner to share in the celebrations. Caleb unfortunately was on duty, but Ian passed on his well wishes and hugs for the kids.

The kids had gotten their pie. Probably more than any child should eat at any one time, but honestly? What was a better reason? He doubted they truly understood what had happened today. Only that they hadn't been made to leave again, and they got to eat all the pie they wanted. Lucy made sure of that.

Will was actually glad David had mostly ruined his first impression by being a homophobic ass. It had been pretty clear his issues weren't appreciated by Mr. Jacks, either. Micah had sat on Will's lap and trembled nearly the entire time David had been passing judgment over them all.

He'd always heard children were good judges of character. Will was positive they had nailed David's perfectly.

Mr. Jacks said he'd get with the judge on Monday to schedule a hearing. He'd warned it might not be anytime soon given the current schedule, but noting what he'd seen today, the children's comfort level, and Will's and Parker's dedication to them, they were all hoping the judge decided in their favor. It was time the kids had a *home*. They lived there now, but it wasn't a home knowing circumstances— much like meeting David and Rita had proved— could change everything for them both in a heartbeat.

Will wanted them to have the security they obviously couldn't have as foster children, in a system that wasn't always going to work in their favor. Trying to put them with someone like David would have been a mistake for everyone.

Parking the car in front of their home, each man wiggled a sleeping child out of their safety seat to carry inside. Groggy efforts to change clothes were followed by at least an attempt to brush teeth before pouring both into their beds.

The strain of the noon meeting followed by the excitement of the impromptu party had worn both kids out. They were sound asleep within seconds of finding their pillows.

"I'm going to call home before it gets much later," Will said. "Let Mom and Dad know we've started the process for the twins."

"They're going to be thrilled. They're officially almost grandparents," Parker murmured a little sleepily. He yawned. "Let me go get the horses taken care of. Be back in a few minutes."

He brushed a light kiss to Will's lips before heading toward the rear door.

Will sat on the edge of their bed, toeing off his shoes with sighs of relief. After a slow stretch, he called his parents in Florida.

When he shared the news, there was about five seconds of shocked silence, then, "Oh my God! You're serious? You're going to do it? What do the kids think of it all?"

He chuckled at her exuberance, saying, "I don't think they really understand. It might take a while." He told her about the meeting with David and Rita and felt her concern and support in her quiet gasps and mutters. "I know that scared them," he said.

"I'm sure it did," she agreed. "Will you let us know when the hearing is? If we can, we'll come out for all of you."

"Thanks, Mom." He knew he wouldn't be able to dissuade her so better to just go with it. "I'm sure the kids would be thrilled to meet their grandparents."

She laughed at that. "We're so happy for all of you."

"Honestly, we are too. It's happening sooner than we planned, but we can't let another scare like today's happen. It killed the twins to have to sit through that thinking they were going to be taken away again."

"They've been through so much," she said.

"I'll call when I know more. I just heard Parker come back in, so I'm going to tell you goodbye."

"Okay, love to all of you."

"You too."

He hung up, smiling, tired, but deep inside happy in ways that he was going to spend the rest of his life enjoying.

Chapter Fourteen

"I'll come for three days," Parker told Kyle through the phone. "I can't take more time than that." Honestly, that was about all he could spare before the kids started school.

He checked the last lock on the barn, tugging on gates as he walked past stalls. In all the mayhem of the day, Parker had missed Kyle's calls.

Parker heard Kyle's grateful acceptance in his tone. "Thank you. Will you let me know when you've made your plans?"

"I have to get a few things here covered, but I'll call."

"I know you don't have to help me, Parker," Kyle said quietly. "I do appreciate it."

"Not doing it for you," he stated before ending the call. Chances were if Kyle was losing money on business, so was Travis, and frankly, he gave way more of a damn about his friend than Kyle.

He couldn't be gone long. Not only would they have to figure out daycare for the kids, but he didn't want to have any possibility that the judge could deny them because he went out of town. He'd have to talk with Mr. Jacks about all of that next week, or have Will do it. If making this trip would leave a black mark on their record, he'd have to find another way to help Kyle. Truthfully, he wished there were a way for everyone to go. Maybe someday.

Once the horses were put to bed, he found Will in their bedroom, drawing off his shirt. With him being unable to see, Parker snuck up in front of him and looped his arms around his husband's waist.

"I better know you," Will joked.

Parker grinned. Warm skin skated under his lips when he bent close.

Will sighed softly, to finish tearing his shirt over his head. It was dropped to the floor and Will's fingers delved into Parker's hair when he spun in Parker's arms.

It had become habit to hang his hat by the door at the end of the day or if he was going to be inside for a while. It was the way he was raised. And he loved the feel of Will's fingers gliding and digging through the strands. Couldn't enjoy that sensation wearing a cowboy hat.

He took his time, coasting with seeking lips and a flicking tongue across a bare shoulder, then upward to playfully tease an earlobe. Will's hands sank low, linking behind his waist. Parker felt the tugs on his shirt and he shifted enough to let Will pull it from his jeans. Once loose, he swept to the front and made short order of the buttons. Will pushed it off shoulders and Parker let it float to the floor.

The tease of skin turned into slow-burning kisses. In socked feet, they sidestepped to the bed's edge. Then jeans and slacks were loosened and dropped from hips. There was a need to reconnect, to have Will against him. To feel the heat of skin and the press of fingers.

The day's ups and downs had taken their toll but now he was able to let the strain and worry, and the fear of losing the kids, go. He knew it wasn't a done deal, but they were one step, several steps closer than they had been when they'd first taken them that morning to Lucy's.

By the time Mr. Jacks had left, Parker was confident they'd made a strong case for the kids. And Will... He leaned to stare into eyes that he adored. Words weren't necessary. Every thought and emotion was on the surface for Parker to see.

Cupping his face between both palms, Parker caressed his lips, prolonging the enjoyment as much as he could. They were both breathing heavily when they came up for air. Moving together, they knelt on the bed, then sank to the mattress wrapped in each other's arms. Kisses lengthened. Fingers roamed and caressed. Parker gasped then moaned when Will's touch lightly grazed over the stiff arousal behind his underwear.

"Want this," Will said, huskily. "Need you."

Parker growled low in his chest. Rolling them over, he stared at Will. Kissing a heated trail over his chest, he wiggled southward, working Will's underwear down with him. Parker removed his while off the bed, then reversed his trip, dropping more slow and suckled kisses to skin.

Will's twitches and panted gasps were growing stronger; his moans, needier. Parker loved the sounds Will made, especially when he paid attention to his dick. Low, growly groans that drove Parker crazy. Prepping his man with patient presses of his thumb relaxed Will's body. Combining the calculated twist and drive of his fingers with cock-swallowing sucks had Will coming apart on the bed. Arching and trying to drive with his hips or push down with his body, absolutely unable to choose one, yet wanting both.

Shimmying with aching slowness up Will's frame a few moments later, he paved his way with scorching kisses until he was centered above him. "Turn over for me," Parker purred, licking like a cat with long strokes over his chest.

Parker gave him room to move and reached for the lube, waiting for him to settle. He ran a palm over Will's butt. A little fuzzy, warm, and so round. A good squeeze earned a sighing smile. Warming the lube on his finger, he eased into Will's channel with a finger, then two, wiggling them to give him the most pleasure.

"God, Parker." He bunched bedding in his hands, arching his spine to push into his touch.

"I know," he crooned.

Satisfied he wouldn't hurt the man he loved, he knelt close and pulled Will's hips up off the bed a bit, tilting to sink into him with a muffled groan. His eyelids closed as pressure swept upward with an electric surge, popping nerves along his spine. Carefully leaning his weight forward, he thrust in with teasingly slow patience. The way Will trembled proved how much he was affected by the speed and intensity.

Braced above Will, he found his hands and wove their fingers together, feeling the heat of skin from his chest to thighs. Tender movements filled Will's channel, the flex and pull a feeling like no other. "Love you," he roughly said, licking beneath Will's ear to add a kiss here and there.

Will's lips were parted, panted breathing all he was capable of. With his eyes closed and sweet kissed to perfection lips, Parker had never seen a more arousing, or beautiful sight. His hips flowed with Parker's, the action timeless, seamless.

It wasn't a rough tumble, it wasn't a needful release.

It was loving perfection.

The wave built, a heartbeat at a time. A tug-of-war that neither man particular cared who won or lost.

The scent of heated skin beneath his nose drove him to burrow into Will's neck, the rush of his pulse a solid tick against Parker's cheek.

Will twisted, hunting for a kiss and Parker gave it to him, languorous and sweet. With a subtle shift of weight, the angle changed and Will's fingers clenched around his, his body thrumming with pleasure.

The pace never really increased, but the intensity burned. Until Will was gasping, shuddering, and thrusting in answer to Parker's loving.

Parker groaned, biting Will's shoulder, shackling them together around his shoulders to sink as deep as he could reach. The pulse filled his length, making him shudder in release when it overcame him. Will's frame twitched, enveloping his, pulling the last of his orgasm from him as he floated from the crest of his own.

Panting, breathless, he rested his head on Will's strong body. "Love you so much," he whispered, swallowing to cure the dryness in his throat.

"Never anyone like you," Will said, sounding a little wispy himself. "Always gonna love you. Always gonna love my cowboy."

Parker's lips twitched at the sleepy words. "Cowboy fetish."

"Yeah," he sighed. "Lucky me. I happen to know one."

Parker's laughter warmed to a lighthearted snicker. "Let's get cleaned up."

Will nodded his agreement.

They enjoyed an unhurried shower, with a lot of smiles and shared kisses before both finally tumbled into bed, curling against one another to fade into sleep.

* * * *

Parker shifted on the bed, but had to stop. Something was poking him in the back. Twisting on his neck, he blinked in the darkness. Twin heads of dark hair were huddled together between him and Will. He had no idea how they'd managed to sneak into the bed without either Will or Parker noticing.

He rolled over onto a shoulder and slipped his arm under the pillow, holding them close. He discreetly tapped Will's head to rouse him.

"I said it was okay," Will offered, drowsily.

Okay, so only Parker had slept through it. He smiled gently. It looked like Chelsea was sound asleep. "Have a bad dream, kiddo?"

Micah burrowed close, a faint watery sniffle evident in his voice. "I thought the angry man took us away."

"Not letting you go," Parker said to Micah, pressing a kiss to the boy's forehead.

Micah nodded, a faint hiccup following.

"Sleep. Family breakfast in the morning." He focused on Will. "How long ago did they come in?"

"About fifteen minutes. Probably why he woke you up. All the movement and bouncing," he said, keeping his voice low.

Parker settled on his pillow. "Probably." Gently flipping his fingers through Micah's hair, he started to hum a tune he could remember his mother singing for him. A locked away memory. Half asleep already, it took mere minutes to get him completely there.

"Gonna make a wonderful dad," Will said huskily when he was done.

"We *both* are," Parker corrected him. "Go to sleep."

Will blew him a kiss and then settled down to drift off.

Chapter Fifteen

Parker pulled underneath the old oak in the front yard, stopping the engine on the rental. A sense of surreal disquiet sank into him, staring at his old home again. He'd only been there once since his father had kicked him out five years ago, and that had been for his father's funeral.

Now, almost a year later, he was back.

He really didn't want to be. He hated leaving the kids behind, hated leaving Will too, already homesick for his family and he'd only been gone since that morning. First he had to drive to Des Moines to catch a flight, and after landing in Galveston, drive to the ranch.

"You're sure there won't be a problem with me going?"

Will shook his head, helping him clean up after dinner two weeks before. "I verified it with two different offices and left a message with Mr. Jacks. Just in case. You can go, the kids can't. Not fair, but rules are rules for a reason."

"Won't be like that forever," Parker said.

"No, not if we get the court's blessing. But until then we have to play their game."

Parker knew he was right. Didn't mean he had to like it though. He'd already called home once, to let them know he'd landed safely. He'd call again in a few hours, closer to bedtime.

Sitting in the car, watching the house, the lack of movement, the lack of sound finally infiltrated. He shivered. It felt like a ghost town. Deserted. Forlorn and unloved.

Grabbing his hat to put on his head, he dug his overnighter out of the trunk and smacked it shut. Not even a dog to greet him. The surrounding silence felt almost like a void in time. Eerie.

Wood under his feet creaked walking to the door, made more noticeable in the utter absence of life and sound.

He knocked and waited. Kyle knew he was coming.

The man looked more haggard than he had when he'd made that drive to Jasper when he finally opened the door.

"Thank you, Parker."

"Like I told you, I'll do what I can, but it might be too late."

"I know." He shut the door. He shuffled around in his sweats and house slippers. Slumped shoulders bowed under a red flannel shirt, tails swaying. "You can have your old room, if you're okay with that? I cleaned it up and put in furniture."

"I guess you took over Dad's room," Parker said, hanging his hat by the door.

"I did, originally. I sleep out here on the couch now." He let his gaze fall away. "I can't sleep in there any longer."

Parker pinched his lips. He didn't *want* to feel sorry for him, but damn it, he did. Letting out a breath, he finally put a hand on Kyle's shoulder. "Let me put this stuff down and I'll meet you in the office."

Kyle nodded and walked with him through the house, separating when Parker opened the room door. The room itself was nothing he remembered. None of his original things remained. The majority had already been removed or destroyed long before he'd arrived for his dad's funeral a year ago.

After dropping his bag on the bed, he retreated and went further down the hall to the second doorway from the end. It was open. Several boxes were sitting on the two chairs, open, and there were ledgers on the desk. Kyle was sitting on the floor with a legal pad at his hip, a calculator on his thigh, and more papers and files scattered around him on the floor.

He ran a hand over his head and down his face. "Man, Kyle. You didn't tell me it was this bad."

He rolled a shoulder. "Bad is bad. I have to find a way to make this work, or I'm homeless."

Parker sighed and entered the room. "Okay." He stacked stuff resting on the desk and found a spot to sit behind it. "Let's see what you've got so far."

Parker helped him reorganize his father's paperwork. It was no small blessing of his own that he'd been taking business courses with Uncle Brice's help, to know what he was looking at, and what he was looking for.

He held up a tax document. "Find me the last five years of this."

Kyle nodded and stood, digging through files, gradually uncovering the pages Parker needed.

Two hours later, he rubbed over his forehead. "Dawson was worth his weight in gold," he muttered, finding yet more gaps and zero balances paid. His dad had more than dropped the ball. He'd completely blown off all responsibility without his right hand man. It was a wonder the electricity was paid on time.

"What was he spending the money on if he wasn't keeping maintenance records or paying taxes?" he asked Kyle. Kyle gave him a blank, tired stare. "He had to be spending the money on something. New bulls? Horses?"

"Not that I ever saw."

"So he was earning, but not spending, and not paying upkeep." He rubbed stiffly over his mouth. "Where are his private account registers?"

"Those are still in the bedroom."

"I need to see those."

"Okay." Kyle creaked standing off the floor. "Damn bones." He shuffled out of the room.

This was taking a chunk of Kyle's soul to fix. The more he uncovered, the more the man was feeling used and betrayed. Parker understood too well. Money that should have been collected and spent on the operation had never made it past his dad's hands. The hole in the ranch's finances was growing, and he was positive his dad had a reason.

He was also beginning to suspect he would need to find a professional to get to the bottom of all of this.

"He was paying his crew, though, right?" he asked Kyle when he returned.

"Yeah. We got our checks." He placed the checkbook on the desk.

Well, that was one good thing. But what the hell did he do with the rest of it?

Another hour of organizing and digging didn't produce a whole lot. His personal bank register revealed even less than the office records. Parker leaned back in the chair, taking in the office. Memories. Overheard words. He frowned, trying to remember. "He had a safe somewhere." His gaze kept flicking, and lingering, to the left.

"He did?" Kyle looked up, blinking blearily. The papers he held in his hand drifted to his lap.

"He never told you?"

"Nope."

Parker stood and studied the bookcase. "This is new for me. How long has it been here?"

Kyle shrugged. "Never really thought about it."

"Help me move it."

Kyle stood and grabbed a side, walking it away from the wall. Setting it down, Parker began hunting, drifting his hand over the wall behind it.

"What are you looking for?"

"A seam. It's just a guess that it's here. It might be in his room too. He never told me, exactly, but I know he had one."

Kyle did the same, running slow fingers over the paneling. He skipped, and went back. "This?"

Parker trailed him, riding the faint seam for about nine inches. "That's it." He smiled. "Now, where is the lock?"

He pushed on each edge and nothing happened. He frowned. "Dad was an asshole. He wouldn't make this easy if it *did* get discovered."

"Maybe it has a remote release?"

"Like an electronic catch?

Kyle nodded.

"Okay, any ideas what?"

Kyle stood, his chin dropping a hair as he thought. "Was there something he always carried?"

"In his pocket?" Parker mused, trying like hell to remember. He ran a hand through his hair. "I was sixteen and it was five years ago."

"He was a secretive SOB. Never gonna argue that."

Parker snickered. *Secrets. Pocket.* Memories of his father filled his brain as he sifted through them. What did he always have on him? What did he never let Parker touch? What? He snapped straight. "Shit! Of course! Where's his belt buckle?"

"His buckle?"

"He guarded that thing like it was made of gold."

"It was gold," Kyle said, not getting it. "It was his last trophy buckle."

"Exactly. He loved that thing more than me," Parker said.

Kyle's eyes shot wide then clouded over. "And me." He growled and spinning on a heel this time, stomped out of the room. "He wouldn't let me touch this, ever. Not even if I offered to polish it. He'd even said once he wanted to be buried with it," Kyle explained with a reawakened fierceness when he returned, the buckle clutched in a hand.

"Well, tough titty. It wasn't in the will, and his ass wasn't here to argue."

Kyle snorted. He handed it to Parker who flipped it and with a finger found the slight bump on the underside. It wasn't a pressure bump, or a button, per se, but something had definitely been inserted into the back and covered. "Okay, there is something there, for sure."

On impulse, he ran the buckle slowly over the seams and like a magic trick, he hit a midpoint and the wall popped open.

"Son of a bitch," Kyle muttered.

"That's being too kind, and insulting to female dogs," Parker offered with a sideways glance. He tossed the buckle to the desk and swung open the panel. The safe sat in front of them. "I feel like James Bond."

Kyle started chuckling.

"We're halfway there, but I'm not a safecracker," Parker said.

Kyle scrubbed stiff fingers through his hair. "Me either." A minute later, he said, "We've found this. Let's do something for dinner and think on how to get it open."

Parker checked his phone. "Yeah, I need to call home to tell the kids goodnight."

He followed Kyle from the office.

"Any ideas on what the combination could be?" Kyle asked once they were sitting at the table with sandwiches. More proof Kyle was holding things together with a shoestring. The kitchen didn't looked like it had been stocked in months.

"Not one," Parker admitted.

Kyle's shoulders slumped. "Me either." He pushed food around on his plate. "How are we going to get into it?"

"Let me call Travis and talk to Dawson. Maybe he'll have suggestions."

"I hope so," Kyle said, morose. He pitched the chip he held to the plate in front of him and planted his face into upright palms. "Going to fucking lose everything. Fucking bastard! You probably don't know this, but your father ruined me. I couldn't buy a dog right now because of what he did to my credit willing me this place."

"Shit," Parker said on a hissed breath. "Seriously?"

"I'm as good as dead if I can't pull this sinking ship up again."

"Will selling it help?"

"Everyone but me," he replied. "I've been selling off the cattle about thirty head at a time, to stay afloat."

"The horses?"

"I have mine. The rest are gone." He pushed away from the table with a stiff arm. "Even if I do get this place rolling again, I'll have to start from scratch." He sagged in his chair. "Maybe I should let it go. If I don't fight it, I can at least walk out of here with my clothes and my horse, and start over somewhere. If I fight for it, I will lose everything if I can't save it."

"Let's see what we can do about the safe. If it doesn't have what we need, I have enough saved up to help you hire someone who can do the work to untangle the finances if that's what we need to do. But I'm only going to do that if you want to save it, and you will pay me back. I'm not going to toss out money to have you walk away." He gathered his hands on the table, resting above the remains of his plated sandwich.

"Why would you even bother?"

"Because frankly, I'd love to see my dad get fucked. So he's not alive to witness it. This ranch was my home, all I knew for sixteen, almost seventeen years. And then the fucker kicked me out. I found something out there I never thought I'd have. Someone who loves me for everything I am, the kind of love that dad didn't have for anyone but himself. For that reason alone, I'm willing to help you. Because if I'd never been kicked out, I would have wound up hating myself for even breathing."

Kyle's chin dipped to his chest. *Direct hit.*

"And you know I'm right," Parker pressed.

"That's still a mess in my head," he said, subdued. "But I'm trying."

"What he did to you was ten times worse than he did to me."

"How do you figure?" Kyle raised enough to meet Parker's gaze.

"Because he let you stay, because he used you every day he was alive. Once I was gone, he had no control over me. I learned to rely on myself, and for the most part, I could, and did. I don't want to know what you and he did, I don't want to know anything about your relationship, but I do know how selfish that man was." He softened his voice. "Tell me the truth. Did he ever, even once, try to make you happy? Did he ever do anything other than take, demand what he could and then take even more from you?"

Kyle swallowed slowly. His eyes grew misty, but not a single tear fell. "No."

"That is why I'm willing to help you," Parker said, gentler. "We all need to know someone gives a damn, even if it's just a friend, a neighbor, or someone you met on the street today."

"After what I did..."

He shook his head. "It took guts to come to me, Kyle." He stood from the chair and cleaned his plate to go into the sink. He patted his shoulder when he went to walk past him. "I hated my dad at the end, and honestly, I still do. The things he did, I will never tell my own kids because they will never know that kind of anger and hate in their lives. So, I guess you could say I'm doing this to get my own revenge. I don't need the ranch, I don't need anything it stood for, either. But you do. So you decide if you have the will and determination to save it. Because I'd love to have that mean fucker spinning in his grave to know two queers saved the land he sabotaged."

Kyle snorted, then wiped a hand over his drawn face.

"Think about it."

Parker gave him a final shoulder shake, then walked out the front door to call home.

Chapter Sixteen

"Hey, cowboy. How's it going?"

Parker leaned on the rail outside with his elbows, gazing out into the quiet with the phone at his ear. "Not great, but we haven't found everything yet." He sighed. "Good to hear your voice."

"You too, sweetheart."

Parker went to mush inside. He missed Will something fierce. "How are the kids?"

"Micah is a little quiet. We're going to watch a movie tonight. Just curl up on the couch with popcorn."

"He's scared I'm not coming home," Parker guessed.

"I think so, too. Hold on. Kids! Pop's on the phone!"

Parker slouched a little, scraping his slow-swinging foot over the porch wood, but hearing Will call for the twins had him smiling in an instant. *Pop.* He wondered if that would be one of those things he never got tired of hearing. He hoped so.

He heard them both chattering and clambering "Me me me!" to talk to him as they got closer— and louder.

"How about we put it on speaker? Is it safe to do that?"

"Yeah, I'm outside and there's no one but me and Kyle. I'll tell you why after."

"Okay." Parker heard the rustle of the phone. "You're on speaker."

"I can't be on speaker. I can't hear a thing from them."

He braced himself with a grinning wince as screams of *Pop!* filled the space between him and the phone, as he held it away from his ear.

He laughed deeply. "Okay, okay, I'm here."

"Where are you?" they chimed almost in unison.

"I'm pretty far away," he told them. "In another state."

"Can we come?" Chelsea begged.

"Sorry, baby. Not this time. But I'll be home soon. Miss you both so much," he said, almost aching. "We'll go to Lucy's for sundaes when I get home. How does that sound?"

Their excited cheering filled the phone again.

"Okay, let me talk to Pop and then we'll watch a movie."

"Yay!"

Parker smiled listening as Will shooed them into the living room.

"Sundaes?" Will joked. "Good thing I know of a dentist for those two."

Parker knew he wasn't really upset. They both spoiled them in their little ways. "They behaving for Jeannie?"

"So far," he answered. "What's going on there?"

Parker gave him the condensed version. "We found his safe, have no idea how to get into it, though."

"What do you think he was doing with the money?"

"A guess? Putting it away for himself." A sweeping look took in the outer buildings and the barn. "It's not falling apart, but I can see a few things

147

that should have been repaired." Lifted shingles on the barn, paint, mainly little things that could be left for *later*. He didn't think it would be a stretch to say that there hadn't been any way for Kyle to do what needed to be done either, not alone, not broke. "Not sure why else he would have been pocketing the money, to be honest."

"How long are you going to stay if you can't figure this out?"

"The three days I promised." He ducked his head. "I don't want to be gone for longer," he admitted. "It's not uncomfortable being here, but..." He blew out a slow breath.

"It's not home," Will said gently.

"No. And I miss all of you." *Even Ian and Caleb.* The rest of his family. It was as though his life started that day he landed in Jasper. "Let me call Travis and see if he can come over tonight. I need to talk to his foreman about Dad's safe."

"Okay, sweetheart. Love you."

"You too." Almost sighing with longing, he ended the call home.

Finding Travis' number, he was next.

"Sure. Can be there in about half an hour," he offered once Parker explained it to him. "Let me find Dawson. He should still be here."

"Thanks. Really appreciate it."

"You know it," he remarked, chuckling. "Always got each other's back."

"Yep. Okay, see you in a few." He heaved a sigh, letting the silenced phone drift downward to rest, bent over his elbows against the rail.

Parker really didn't have any idea of what they were looking for to crack his dad's safe. His father hadn't taken him into his confidences like that back then, *and probably never would have,* he mused. "Selfish bastard." And it was really only a hope that what Kyle needed would be in it. Either the missing funds or the location of them. If it was another dead end, he didn't have a lot of other suggestions. At sixteen, what did it matter to him what his dad did in that office? They sure as hell weren't that kind of close. And there really wasn't that much he remembered from five years ago, either. He'd tried his best to forget after the first two years walking the roads. It was a life that was gone. He wasn't ever going back to it, and after Jasper, he hadn't wanted any part of Texas. With Will and the kids waiting for him, definitely not now.

He had everything he needed at home.

Parker twisted a hair when the front door opened behind him. Kyle shuffled out onto the porch with him.

"Is he coming?"

Parker nodded. "Travis will be here in a bit with Dawson."

Kyle gripped the porch rail beside him. "Thank you." Silence drifted between them for a few minutes. Kyle leaned on crossed elbows, both staring out over the spread of land between the house and barn. "I really don't understand all of why you want to help me, but I've been madder than hell at Chet, then so defeated, I did almost pack up and walk away."

Parker twisted to face Kyle. "What did you do?"

"I drove to talk to you. This ranch is my home." He cleared his throat, staring forward. "I know you don't want to know, but you should know a little." He clasped his hands and bowed his head. "I made the mistake of thinking he cared, maybe making a fantasy out of it all. I don't know." He seemed to grow smaller between his shoulders. "Things didn't happen between us until at least a year after he'd done that to you. I think it was a matter of loneliness on both our parts more than anything. And hell, I found out I was very willing." He snorted derisively. "I guess I've always known I liked men, though I could with women, y'know?"

Parker nodded. "Being with a woman doesn't get your ass kicked." Personal experience on that one.

"Exactly," he said, roughly. "Anyway." He picked at slivers of dry wood fiber on the rail distractedly. "I wasn't expecting what happened that first time, and the more he asked for, the more I thought..." His eyes shut. "Well, you know what I thought. What he was doing was setting me up, getting what he wanted on the side on top of it without ever having to work for it, or woo a woman either. I made it too fucking easy," he muttered. "You'll never know how low I felt the day I found out what he'd done, after the way I treated you and Will at his funeral. It took everyone leaving to make me see it. That was when I started really going through his things. Part of me did want to find anything of yours and get it to you. What's yours is yours. And then I found the trap he set for me." A fist formed and he hit the rail once. "And like a fool, I fell for it hook, line, and sinker."

Parker studied him. His dad did a real number on Kyle. The arrogance he'd seen at his dad's gravesite was long gone. He stood beside a beaten man. "Which is why I'm here. I do know. He was my dad, he wasn't a father. Have you decided what you want to do?"

He dipped his chin. "If we can get into the safe, and it has what we need, or something to get us there, I'll fight, but I'm not going to take your money, or your time from your own family to save this place if it's a dead end. I can find another spread to work on. I'd hate to see it go, but I'm not going to kill myself over it."

"Because he wins."

Kyle nodded slowly. "He does. And honestly, it was what he was going to do no matter how his days came. He was stealing from us all in the end." He pointed to the barn's roof. "Stuff like that kept getting pushed to the back burner."

"I saw that," Parker agreed.

"I'd tell him, and he'd write it down, forgotten until it was brought up again. He was frustrating, but he always said it would be on the next overhaul list, which never happened."

"I wonder if he was going senile. Hoarding is common."

"Is that possible?"

Parker snorted. "Like I'd know? The last day I saw any of this I was three days shy of seventeen. Now, I wonder if being gay was just a way to get rid of me, to not compete with him for what he had planned for the money."

"Anything's possible."

They both lifted their heads when a dust plume on the driveway drew their gazes. "Travis is here." They straightened, waiting for Travis to stop the truck. Dawson climbed out with him, both walking to meet them.

Dawson held out a hand to Parker. "Good to see you, boy."

"You too, old man." He smiled at the friendly teasing.

Dawson nodded in greeting, saying, "Kyle."

"Thank you for coming, Dawson."

"Let's go inside and we'll tell you what we've found," Parker explained. Kyle turned and led the four into the house.

"Everything okay?" Travis asked quickly, quietly.

Parker held back a pace. "As it can be. We'll see if this, if Dawson can help."

Travis shut the door lastly. "Here if you need anything."

Parker smiled at his friend and then they both walked to Chet's office to catch up to the other two.

Chapter Seventeen

Dawson stood before the safe when they walked in, his chin in cupped fingers.

"Do you know it?" Parker asked.

"I'm trying to remember. I never knew the combination, but I knew the old fart well enough, I think I can figure it out."

Kyle snorted. He sat at the desk, his head cushioned on bent arms. "I've already tried the obvious ones, his birthday, the phone number, the house address, and any mix of those I could think of." He spoke without lifting his head from the desk.

"No, it wasn't that obvious," Dawson mused.

"How long did he have it?" Parker wondered.

"He had the wall work done when you were about eight or nine, I guess, so at least since then," Dawson offered, in a remembering tone.

"So what was big in his life then, or the last big thing?"

Travis came in and hunkered down in a chair, patiently waiting.

Dawson twisted at the waist. "Can I have a pen and paper?"

Kyle straightened, shuffled things on the desk, and handed over the items to Parker, who gave them to Dawson.

Dawson began scribbling notes. "His last ride was when he was..." He glanced at Parker. "Doing math," he muttered thoughtfully. Parker snickered.

He wrote down something. "So the year, his age..." He glanced at the combination wheel. "Okay, only up to sixty." He mumbled, writing. "Let me try this."

He spun the wheel then wrote down a few more things. The man had patience neither Parker or Kyle had. He also had light fingers. He smiled when he nailed the first number on the second try. "Got you now, you old fuck."

He spun the wheel to clear it, and rolled out a combination and pulled the lever. It popped open.

"How?" Parker asked, amazed.

"There were certain things that bastard was proud of like a beauty pageant queen's bygone days. His last ride was one of them. The combination is that score, divided in half, and his riding number." He pointed to a frame on the wall. It was a collection of his numbers, ticket stubs, and a couple photos of him receiving his trophy along with the belt buckle that had unlocked the wall partition to get to the safe.

"Fucking hell. How'd we miss that?"

"Parker would have been too young to know, and you weren't here," Dawson said, offering a shrug of unconcern. "For months after that last ride, he made sure everyone knew that he'd made champion."

"I remember," Parker said. He leaned against the desk and crossed his arms. "Learned quick where I stood with the old man after that, too." Giving up riding seemed to put all his father's focus on Parker instead of shoving it off on riding bulls.

Dawson frowned. "He was too fucking rough on you."

"You never saw him do it, just the bruises afterward. It was my word against his, and even if someone did say something, there were enough men on this ranch scared of him and of losing their jobs to agree with anything a kid would say."

Dawson snorted. "I wasn't one of them. We fought, a lot. Those days he stayed inside because he had a hangover? Those weren't hangovers. You were in school most of the time, so you missed a good bit." He dropped the pad with the written numbers on the desk. "I tried, Parker. I wish I'd done more."

"You tried. That's all anyone can ask for."

He nodded. "Good luck with what's in there."

Parker glanced to Kyle. He'd paled, staring at the opened safe. "Thank you, Dawson."

Dawson cupped Parker's shoulder. "Don't be a stranger, kid."

"Travis has the address in Iowa. I want an invitation to the wedding."

"Be glad to have you."

Parker straightened and they shook hands again. "I'll call before I head home, Travis."

"Better," he warned, reaching his feet. "We'll show ourselves out."

"Thank you both," Kyle said.

They gave dual head nods before they left through the office door. A moment later, the front door opened and closed.

"You ready for this?" Parker asked.

"Not in the least," he said, sounding a little dry and nauseated.

"Better now than later. Get it over with. May change everything, or nothing."

"I know. That's what I'm scared of," Kyle admitted. Shakily, he stood from behind the desk and joined Parker in front of the wall safe. Parker tugged the door all the way open. Inside laid a stack of papers, a small box, and a wall of cash bundles deep.

"Son of a bitch," Kyle gasped.

Parker reached inside for the folders. "Grab the cash. It needs to be counted to see if that could be the sum of what you're short."

"I— You get it. Give me those. I don't want to touch it."

Parker's brow tightened but he handed over the files and gathered up the wrapped bills. Hundred dollar bills in straps. He counted them in his head as he gathered them in his hand.

"Well, it seems to be everything you're short, but this, without counting it, is over three hundred thousand." Parker shook his head at the money, steadying it on the desk.

"Un-fucking-believable." Kyle was trembling, his eyes wide. "I've never seen that much money for real."

Parker shrugged and pushed it to the center of the desk. "Well, it's yours."

"No!" He shrank back from it. "Chet stole that money from the ranch. It's the ranch's, or yours."

Parker sighed. "Let's see the files."

"Put that back in the safe for now." Kyle was avoiding the money like it was the plague.

"Sure." Parker restacked it and blocking the safe so it wouldn't shut, swung the heavy door closed, to put it out of sight. "Better?"

Kyle let out a breath. "Thanks."

They spread out the files on the desk and began reading through the documents. Kyle cupped his chin and left his hand there as his face paled further. "This... This is yours. There's no way I'm taking this as part of the ranch. It wasn't in the will, and he never intended it to be."

He spun the file and handed it to Parker. He did his best to control his shock. His father had invested several sums of his winnings. What he'd intended to do with it all, the money in the safe, the investments, Parker couldn't begin to guess, but there was no doubt, he was staring at a *lot* of cash.

"But the funds can go back into the ranch." He held up a hand, stilling Kyle's next argument. "Let's see what we're legally supposed to do. First, we need to get someone in here who can handle the taxes and get that paid. We also need to see where that money is supposed to be used. It came from the ranch, that much we know." He motioned toward the safe to indicate which he meant.

Kyle grudgingly bobbed his head. "You're right," he said. He glared at the safe. "I just... I've said a lot of things about your dad, and you. I obviously had you both wrong."

Parker grinned and rolled a shoulder. "It's okay. It's a headache, sure, but you've also found the means to not lose your home."

Kyle scrubbed over his face with stiff palms. "Will you stay until I get someone hired to handle this?"

"I'll stay like I said I would."

Kyle showed the first sign of relief Parker had seen since he'd arrived. "Thanks."

"We'll look into getting someone tomorrow."

Kyle didn't complain against the suggestion.

* * * *

Parker woke up to his phone buzzing at him. He slapped his hand around, hunting for it on the bedside table. "Hello?" he grunted.

"Parker, we have a problem."

He shoved up to an elbow, rubbing over his face, trying to wake up. "What? What's wrong?"

"I just got a phone call from Mr. Jacks. Someone has filed a complaint against us, about the kids."

"What?" He jerked up a little straighter, more awake than he wanted to be and definitely not for a good reason.

"He swears it's just a bump, but the judge will have to look into it before he moves forward."

"What does that mean?" He swung his legs over the edge of the bed, holding his head.

"An advocate will be by in the next few days to talk to all of us. You have to come home."

"I will. When are they coming?"

"I don't know. That's the worst part."

Parker could tell Will was very worried about this, the way his voice pitched and lowered.

"Are the kids there right now?"

"No, Jeannie picked them both up on time."

"Okay." He took a slow breath. "Let me wake up, call Mr. Jacks, and then I'll get the last details here taken care of. I'll try to catch a flight tonight."

His gush of relief was unmistakable. "Love you, cowboy."

"Love you too. I'll call in a few hours to check in." He ran a hand through his hair, rubbing into his scalp. He might even break down and get coffee this morning.

"Okay."

They said their goodbyes and he stood, dropping his phone to the bed. "Fucking hell." He dressed and used the restroom, aiming for the kitchen. "Morning," he said in greeting to Kyle.

He nodded. "There's coffee."

"I think I will." He felt awful that just twelve hours ago he'd told Kyle he'd stay, and now he might have to leave within the next eight hours. He wanted to talk to the kids' lawyer first.

"Will just called."

Kyle faced him, sipping at a hot mug.

"You know we're adopting the kids." Kyle nodded. "Someone has filed a complaint. I need to call their lawyer, but I may have to leave this afternoon."

Kyle started to panic. "But... What...? The money?"

Parker raised a hand and Kyle popped his mouth shut. "We'll figure that out. No one will think you had anything to do with what's in the office. I don't. I know it was Dad's doing. You're not going to lose the house." He finished making a coffee for himself, to have something to do with his hands.

He bowed his head. "I just don't know what to do."

"You'll figure it out. One day at a time."

"I don't even know if anyone will work for me, here, again."

Parker put a hand on Kyle's shoulder. "They will. People need the work. You can start mending fences by apologizing to Travis. Little steps. The first thing you need to do is accept everything Dad told you is wrong. You're not wrong, bad, or whatever he made you believe for liking men." He sipped his coffee, licking his lips when the sugar hit him. Will teased him when he did have coffee, because he almost made it coffee-flavored candy. "When you're being honest with yourself, you can be honest with the world, and people will respect that."

"How'd you figure so much out?"

"Life doesn't care about age. It hits you every day."

Kyle sighed. "True." He stared at his coffee. "Okay. Let's take care of as much as we can, so if you have to scoot, you can."

Parker studied him. "I know you're scared, but you're already fixing things. You're going to be fine."

"Am I?"

Parker just smiled. Kyle's expression proved he thought Parker had more faith in him than he did.

Chapter Eighteen

Kyle hung up the phone, looking forlorn and worn down. "The accountant will be here on Monday."

"Good!" They'd spent the better part of the morning organizing his dad's office, his paperwork, and files. The cash and files they'd discovered the day before were inside the safe. Neither had really felt like dealing with it.

"Hey, did you want to see what that little box was?" Kyle asked motioning to the safe.

Parker shrugged. "I guess." He doubted it was anything he really wanted, or needed to know.

Kyle went to the safe and reached inside, withdrawing the small box. It was about four inches square and two inches thick, made of wood with a hinged top. "That's pretty," Kyle said. "What do they call it when it's burned like that? Burn art, or something?"

"I think you're right." The symbol was a Texas emblem and state star on polished wood. "It looks handmade." Parker set it before him on the desk. "Might leave that open. If this is more of that stuff, I'm not doing anything with it." Until he knew where the ranch stood, he didn't want anything. He'd made it this far without anything from his father. He wasn't going to start.

He peeled the lid open. The hinge was a little stiff from not being used, dragging with a raw squeak. Kyle stood at his shoulder, peeking with curiosity.

"What's that?" he murmured.

"Looks like jewelry." Parker started pulling out the pieces.

"Your Mom's?"

"Maybe." Parker pulled out several rings, a wedding set among them, three necklaces and a few pairs of earrings.

"Wonder why'd he keep 'em," Kyle said.

Parker rolled a shoulder. Another one of those *who knows* type of questions. "I guess keep it all in the safe for now. If it was all Mom's, then either she left it behind, or he took them from her."

Kyle shook his head. "One of them had good taste," he remarked, poking at the diamond earrings. "Is there a way to find out if they were your mother's?"

"Not really." He started putting the pieces back into the little wooden box. "Put it with the rest of it, I guess."

Kyle tried to refuse. "You should take at least that much. Odds are they were your mom's. He wouldn't have had any reason to hold on to a woman's stuff."

"Did he ever bring a woman here?"

Kyle scratched his neck, thinking. "Not that I can recall seeing." He cleared his throat. "He didn't need a woman," Kyle offered bitterly. "He had a whore living in his own bunkhouse."

Parker glanced up. "Kyle, don't be like that. That bastard used you."

"Yeah, but I had to be willing to be used," he said. "I'm going to get some coffee." He stepped away a pace and walked from the office.

Parker let him go, knowing Kyle was a messed up wreck thanks to the bullshit Chet had done to him. Mentally, he was a wreck. Physically, he was a husk of a man. It was going to take time for him to find himself again.

Checking the time, Parker stood from behind the desk and walked toward the front of the house. "I'll be outside for a few minutes. Going to call the kids' lawyer."

Kyle gave him a slow head nod. "I'm going to call Travis' place. See if he'd like to share a beer or something this weekend."

Parker gave him a gentle smile. "You can do this, Kyle."

"God, I fucking hope so," he mumbled, sipping at his coffee.

Parker walked through the door for the porch, tugging his phone from his rear pocket.

* * * *

Will stood at the front door of their house, watching the road, following Parker's approach until he stopped beside the house and turned off the car. His legs felt shaky, his heart racing. He wouldn't argue that he was terrified. Just having Parker home again helped. They were a team. He needed his cowboy.

Parker reached his feet, shut the door, and met Will halfway, engulfing him between his arms. "Missed you," Will whispered, his voice thick.

"Missed you too." Parker arched and kissed Will, deeply.

Strong arms that never wavered held Will securely.

"Needed that. The kids here yet?"

"No. Jeannie said she'd give them dinner tonight."

Parker grinned. "I swear those two." He rested his forehead to Will's head. "Then we better get inside. Won't have long to be loud."

Will barked a laugh. "Trying to distract me."

"Yep. Completely."

Will finally relaxed into Parker's chest. "If we lose them," he said, almost choking up.

"We're not going to lose them. They start school next week. They're settled, safe, and happy. Some moron filed a complaint. We both know who it was," he remarked with a growl in his voice.

"Yeah." Will nodded. "I know." There weren't many who knew enough about either of the guys or the kids to attempt any kind of a dissent to stop the adoption.

"And once the judge sees that, realizes the connection, the complaint will be so much dust. We've made every appointment, never failed an inspection. We're on solid ground." He cupped Will's face between his palms. "They want to be here. That right there, says everything."

"Now I know how you felt when I had to tell you about meeting David and Rita." He closed his eyes, too happy to wallow in Parker's support. "I had no idea just how much they'd grown to be ours until that phone call."

"You hadn't completely given yourself the freedom to feel like their dad until we filed," Parker guessed.

"No, I guess I hadn't." Will let out a low sigh. The chance that what did happen, *would* happen, had never been far from his mind. He'd only hoped it wouldn't, until it did and by then, the meeting was out of his hands. "Let's go inside. Jeannie is being a sweetheart to keep them for a little longer tonight."

Parker's lips twitched into a beguiling smirk. The one Will knew and loved. "I do believe I can fill the time."

"God, I'm hoping so."

Parker held him, giving him one more kiss, one packed with everything Will was feeling, and hoping for in the next hour or so.

He released Will long enough to get his overnighter from the trunk. Hauling the strap over a shoulder, he and Will walked up to the door. He hung his hat on the peg then both aimed for the bedroom.

Parker's bag hit the floor and he was reaching for Will as soon as the bedroom door closed.

Will dug his fingers into Parker's hair, holding him close. Parker's kiss was heaven. Strong arms wound around his frame and held him chest to chest. Harsh panting from both had them rocking in a rhythm into one another. Parker's kiss was unlike anyone else's, strong and fierce, caring and tender, and everything in between. "Love you," Will gasped when Parker released him to suck on his neck below his ear.

"Best thing that's ever happened in my life," Parker said, his voice rough with longing.

"Naked. Need you." Will dropped his hands to start tugging on shirt buttons, slipping them quickly apart. Parker shrugged the shirt off his shoulders and Will aimed for his belt and buckle. A couple of hard tugs had it loose and then Will was digging beneath denim to grasp Parker's dick.

Parker groaned, a heavy shudder rolling over his frame. That reaction made Will feel like the luckiest man on the planet. That his touch— *just*— his touch— could make Parker feel like that. Parker reached for his lips, sharing in getting naked as fast as was possible.

Will spun them to push Parker to sit on the edge of the bed. Once there, he jerked off boots and socks, taking jeans down with them. Will was past words, stripping like clothes were liquid, to get body to body. He dove over Parker, rolling them both on the bed.

Parker grabbed his hands and pinned him to the mattress, staring down at him. "It's going to be okay." He pressed his body into Will's, into the bed.

Will stared at him, feeling off balance, almost desperate. Parker's calm began to infiltrate and he drew a slow breath. His heart was racing like a jet engine. A shiver followed the next exhale. He was becoming a muddled mess.

"That's better," Parker murmured a few minutes later, smiling. He released a hand to pet Will's hair and temple. "In this together. Love you. We both love those kids. And they know that." He touched lightly to Will's lips. "And right now, I'm going to make love to you."

Will's skin tightened hearing that. It was exactly what he needed, what he wanted. He swallowed around the lump in his throat. He loved this man to the ends of the earth. Unable to speak, he threaded his free hand into the loose hair on Parker's head and tugged him low, caressing his lips into a kiss that would have melted the icecap.

Parker's moan bordered on wild.

Will splayed his legs invitingly, aching with need to feel Parker against him. A slow rocking of hips told Will he'd gotten the message. Wriggling his caged hand free, he slid down Parker's side until he reached firm roundness and grasped.

Parker was definitely getting the message if the devouring heat of his kiss was any sign. A stretched arm opened the drawer beside the bed, dropping the bottle on the bed next to Will.

Parker grazed over his jaw with kisses, urging Will to let him reach more skin. Shivers fed downward from each kissed spot. It was a slow journey, traveling from Will's chin to his stomach, but it was one Parker clearly enjoyed making, dropping tender kisses and gentle nips of teeth along the way.

Panting, floating in the delicious sensations, he jolted when wet heat collided with the stiff cock waiting for Parker's magic touch. He groaned, wallowing in the oral adoration. A light press at his entrance made him twitch, but he quickly relaxed, longing for the connection that was promised by that touch.

Parker slowly glided down Will's length as he pressed deeper, filling his channel and taking his length as far as he could go. Will was flying, tossed between the flick of his tongue and the twist of fingers as Parker lovingly got him ready.

He whined when Parker seemed to take longer than he had the patience for.

A light chuckle was followed by a suctioned lick and Parker slurping over the flushed tip. Loving hands brought Will's legs high, teasing him with the scrape of nails over skin.

He tried to scoot closer, craving. Parker finally relented, meeting him on the bed. Holding his length, he pushed against Will's flexing body.

"God," he groaned as Parker began to fill him. He locked his arms beneath his knees, rolling with the press of Parker's hips.

Parker's eyes glittered with a loving desire when Will locked gazes with him. Everything he felt lay open like a book in those moments. He hid nothing from Will. One of the many reasons he loved this man the way he did.

Parker pulled back until he was almost free, then slowly corkscrewed his hips, filling Will with a controlled patience that made him want to scream.

"Parker!" He had less control than his lover, obviously.

Parker grinned, then began to shatter Will, thrusting and pumping with building urgency. There was no sense of where one ended and the other began. They were in this together. Feeling the pleasure, feeling the heat of their bodies where they connected. It was a sensation unlike anything Will had ever known, or ever would again.

Will grasped at Parker, urging him. "Close, sweetheart." His eyes rolled into his head when Parker shifted, hiking his hips just enough to roll over nerves. He knew he wouldn't last. Not with Parker doing that.

When Will adjusted to grasp his dick, Parker braced his leg for him, a slight stutter in his movement his only sign that he was watching Will's hand on his own cock. His heart pounded, matching Parker's intensity. He groaned, flexing in sheer pleasure, then stroked his cock in his hand.

Parker's thrusts became choppy, driven. Will gasped, groaning as heat surged, rolling over his body. Pressure was building, roaring down his spine to collide with the waves of heat. He trembled beneath it all.

His vision was filled with Parker. The glitter of his eyes, the flush on his face. "Love you," he rasped, panting. Parker flexed forward, finding Will's lips for a heated kiss, moaning deeply, arching with his thrusts.

"Will." He gasped and lurched, and Will almost cried out with the flash of heat.

It took him barely heartbeats to follow, spurting onto his chest between them. Sparks flared along nerves and he swung his free arm upward, capturing Parker to hold him tight.

Parker nuzzled under his ear a few minutes later, both their breathing finally slowing to normal. "Love you so much."

"Love you, Parker," he said, his voice dry.

Parker shifted and Will took a moment to peek at the clock. "I suppose our free time is about over."

Parker grinned, pressing it into Will. "Let's go shower." He lipped lightly at an earlobe. "We can sneak in another fifteen minutes that way."

Will chuckled warmly, too happy for words. He had Parker, the twins were due home, and he knew he was loved by all of them. For this moment, everything was perfect.

Chapter Nineteen

Parker held Chelsea's hand walking up the stairs of the courthouse. Will glanced toward him above the kids, holding Micah's hand in his. The moment of truth. Neither had been able to fully hide their worry over the coming day. The twins were subdued, but calm. They knew as well as the adults what today was about. And until it was done and sealed with the gavel, no one was going to be at ease. They paused at the top of the stairs.

"Thanks for being here," Will said to his parents when they reached them.

His mother fussed over him then gave him a hug. "Of course we'd be here for this! I'm more surprised the whole of Jasper didn't follow."

Parker snickered. "Caleb and Ian wanted to."

"As did the girls," Will added. "We thought it would be less traumatic if things..."

Will's dad shook his head. "Not going to happen. Positive son. Be positive." He cupped him on the upper arm in support.

Parker saw the kids eyeing the older couple curiously.

"Chelsea, Micah, these are my parents. Today, they will become your grandparents," Will explained.

Chelsea's eyes were wide. "Really?"

Both Parker and Will nodded.

"Let's go get the judge's okay so we can go to breakfast, as a family," Will's mother stated firmly, adding a smile.

All six filed through the heavy doors, and approached the guards and metal scanners.

"One at a time," the guard intoned. "Please remove all metal buckles, cell phones, wallets, and satchels for the scanner."

Parker shook Chelsea's hand. "You want to go first? Make sure I do it right?" He slid his belt free and laid it in the bucket for the X-ray machine. His phone went with it. He patted his pockets and quickly dropped his wallet with it all.

She stared at him, then nearly smiled, being brave. She walked through, her head held high. "Okay, Pop, your turn." Parker knew they'd done this enough times, making her feel like she was important would help them all through this.

The guard waved him through. Her smile brightened when he joined her on the other side.

Parker watched as the others did the same, Mrs. Parkinson letting them do a search of her purse as well. It took as long to get inside the building as it did to sit through the hearing, he groused mentally. Once everyone was dressed and put back together, he turned off his phone. He waited while the others did also.

He missed his hat reaching for his hair, but it was in the car. No point in bringing it in when it was impolite to wear it indoors to begin with.

"Do we know which room?" Mr. Parkinson asked.

"Judge Barton's rooms?" Will asked to confirm.

"Two-twelve. That hallway." The guard pointed.

"Thank you."

They turned and started in that direction. And they all stopped dead when Mr. Jacks appeared around the next corner.

David was with him.

Mr. Jacks shook his hand and David left the building, without giving a single glance of recognition in their direction. Chelsea had squeezed in closer and Parker cupped a palm to her shoulder, holding her protectively until the other man was gone.

"Mr. Parkinson. Mr. Vandersoot."

"Was that anything we need to worry about?" Will asked.

"Not any longer." He moved to the side and gestured. "The judge is waiting for us."

"Are we all allowed in the courtroom?" Mr. Parkinson asked.

"Certainly. They'll be called up and asked a few questions and the judge will give his ruling on their petition." He smiled kindly. "Don't let seeing him cause you any concern."

"We know he made the complaint," Parker said quietly.

"Those are anonymous," Mr. Jacks pointed out evenly. "I can't say if it was or not."

Parker dropped it. Sometimes facts were too evident to be anything else.

The building was echo-y and felt like it had been built in the last century. A lot of stone and marble with heavy wooden doors. Parker didn't know if it was merely his perception or if it was truly the intent, but it gave him a very ominous feeling to be in that building.

The courtroom double doors stood wide as they approached. There were a few benches already filling. Both kids huddled closer as they took in the room.

"Let's sit over there." Will motioned to a completely empty row. "We can all be together."

Parker agreed, letting Will's parents in to sit first, so Will, Parker, and the twins would be able to slip out when it was time for them to face the judge.

Each man embraced a kid closely. "It's going to be okay," Parker heard Will say to Micah. He was hiding in Will's chest, refusing to relax. Not that Parker blamed him. Every time they were in that courtroom, their entire life was put into a tailspin. "They're not going to take you away from us. We're here to make us a real family."

God, I hope so. Parker shared a wary look with Will. Until it was done, he just couldn't believe it was going to be that easy.

People were talking in quiet tones around them, a few coming and going before the top of the hour when the doors would close.

A few minutes later, a bailiff closed the doors, and "All rise" was announced.

Parker drew a slow breath as Judge Barton entered.

Chelsea crawled into his lap then tucked into his shoulder when they sat again. Micah did the same with Will. He wanted to burst from the room and run far with those two kids.

He made himself stay as calm as he could. If Chelsea or Micah had even a hint of how terrified he was for them, for all of them…

The bailiff called a case number. Mr. Jacks tapped Parker on the shoulder. "That's us." He wasn't even aware of how much time had passed.

He nodded, nudging Chelsea off his lap. The four followed the kids' advocate to the front of the room.

Judge Barton read over the file in front of him. Parker did his best to not fidget while they waited. The kids were actually doing better than he was.

The judge finally looked up to address them, studying each in turn. "Mr. Parkinson. Mr. Vandersoot. Thank you for being here today." He knitted his fingers together to rest on the file. "As I'm sure you're aware, when you undertake a foster contract, you're already being given the highest regard possible for the child, or," he smiled for the two youngsters, "children. While it's not unheard of to have first time fosters adopt, it isn't very common, either. I have to think that given the situation, you've both put a sincere amount of thought into this request." He focused on Will, which silently, Parker was relieved for. He'd never done well with authority figures.

"Your Honor," Will started. "Parker and I knew the restrictions and time limitations that came with being foster parents. That this situation, or any, would, under most circumstances, be temporary." He glanced to Parker, who nodded just so. "However, given our mutual desire to be more, to be a family, fostering was a valid way to offer our home as well as test ourselves." He took a slow breath, speaking clearly. "When Micah and Chelsea came to us, they were very unsure, and in some ways, terrified, with due cause. What we've seen in the months since they've come into our lives are two children who love their aunts and uncles and are adored in return. Who are excited about starting school with an actual class, with kids their own age. Two children who are adapting well to the rules of our house, as a family." This time, he looked down at both children and smiled so tenderly, Parker's eyes watered. "Two kids who bring a light into our house, along with the messy bathroom and the crazy spaghetti nights." Micah actually giggled, slapping a hand over his face before staring wide-eyed at the judge.

Parker caught the slightest flicker of a smile ghost over the judge's face, which Will missed watching Micah trying to control himself.

"So, saying we've given this due consideration? Every day since we were asked to give them the safety and support they needed. We knew two weeks after they'd arrived that we could do more, and if they were willing, would continue to do so much more for the rest of their lives, and ours."

"I see." The judge stared at the children. Chelsea raised her chin, not balking at his scrutiny. Parker's chest heated with pride. That had been a long time in coming for them both. "They've made incredible progress being in your care." He looked down and thumbed through the paperwork, stopping at a single sheet. "There was a complaint report filed, but I also met the person behind it. After discussing it with Mr. Jacks, I'm going to dismiss the complaint report. Every visitation and home visit went with superb recommendations from our advocates. Another commendable effort. I want to ask the kids now... Chelsea? Are you happy in Jasper?"

She looked up to Parker who nodded for her to answer. "Very much, sir."

"Very respectful, young lady," he remarked. "And both Mr. Vandersoot and Mr. Parkinson are good to you?"

She nodded but Parker squeezed her hand to encourage her to speak. "Yes, sir."

The judge turned to Micah. "And Micah. Are you happy staying with these two men?"

"Yes, sir," he said, not quite as boldly as Chelsea, but still clearly.

"And you both know if I grant their petition, you become their children? Son and daughter?"

Both children nodded.

"Let the record show both children motioned in agreement," he said to the aide. He studied the file one more time, then grabbed his pen and signed something. He replaced the pen with his gavel. "Then I hereby grant your petition, gentlemen. What I see today are two children who are blossoming under your care and guidance. The children I saw on that bench previously are gone. And I must say, I wish all had that gift."

He tapped the gavel to the sound block and both Chelsea and Micah jumped.

Mr. Jacks touched Will and Parker on the shoulder and herded them all out of the courtroom, Will's parents following.

"So that's it?" Will asked. He sounded as mystified as Parker felt.

Mr. Jacks was beaming. "That's it. The judge has signed it, and made it legal. All you need to do is decide whose name you want first on the adoption paperwork."

Parker sniffled. "It's real?" *That was it?*

Will bent down and hugged a shocked Micah. "Baby boy! You're ours!"

Micah squealed, then Chelsea squealed. "Me! I want up!" She raised her arms, hopping around with boundless energy now that the hard part was over. Having to be still and quiet.

Parker scooped her up and swung her around. When he stopped, Will gathered everyone, his parents included, for a huge group hug, right there in the hallway, uncaring of any passerby as smiles grew and eyes glistened as it all sank in.

"A family," Will offered. "Dad, Pop, Chelsea, and Micah."

"I like the way that sounds," Will's mom said, dabbing at her eyes with a tissue.

"So proud of both of you," his dad added. "And now we have grandchildren to spoil." He grinned, roughing Will's hair with a hand. "Grandkids."

"And a cat," Micah chipped in.

"Can't forget Tinker, can we?" Will remarked.

"Nope." He shook his head hard.

"Love you both so much." Will kissed them with loud emphasis. He got a riot of giggles from both.

"I wish I could stay a little longer, but I have another court appointment to make," Mr. Jacks explained.

"Thank you so much for all you've done." Will shook his hand without losing Micah. Parker did the same. "Couldn't have done it without you."

"You're the two who did this, well you two and Chelsea and Micah. You make a wonderful family."

Will leaned close and Parker dared a quick kiss, then the group said their goodbyes to Mr. Jacks.

"So, now what?" Parker asked.

"Who's hungry?" Will's dad asked.

Both kids cried out "Me!"

"Well, there you go," Will said, chuckling. They strolled down the hall and back out the front doors, bypassing the security lane to leave.

"Oh my God," Parker gasped. He stopped, frozen outside the building's doors as the others poured out around him into the sunlight. At least a dozen people stood on the steps holding signs with Will's, Parker's,

Chelsea's, and Micah's names on them in bold, bright colors and designs.

"Dad!" Will cried. "Who were you working with?"

Ian and Caleb moved forward from the front of the crowd, carrying a broad banner between them. "We put him up to it," Ian admitted, grinning like a fool.

"And if it hadn't gone right?" Will asked briskly.

Ian and Caleb shared a confused look. "That didn't even occur to us," Ian said. "Won't say it was guaranteed, but we never doubted you two."

Parker ducked his head, all but hiding in Chelsea's hair.

Ian's touch on his shoulder had him blinking, pulling up to look into his understanding gaze. "You're *our* son, Parker, where it counts," he said thickly. "And now we have a niece, Chelsea, and a nephew, Micah." He cradled both as he said their name, a gentle hand to their heads where they were still being held by Pop and Dad. "And they're never going to be without family again."

Tears fell down Parker's cheeks. "Love you both," he choked out.

Ian leaned close, touching foreheads. "You too."

"Does this mean we can have pie again?" Chelsea asked.

"How about we have lunch first this time?" Will asked. "Then we can have pie."

Micah and Chelsea both nodded hard, which got a rowdy laugh from the gathered crowd.

Epilogue

Chelsea held Pop's hand as he guided her down the hallway. It was loud and kids were everywhere. Signs were scattered on the walls. No bullying. Be kind. Speak softly. She knew a lot of those, and what they meant. There were just as many adults as kids, which seemed odd. Didn't just kids go to first grade? They paused in the hall as Dad stopped and said, "Okay, Micah. This is your room. Chelsea? You see where he's going to be, right?"

She nodded. "Mr. Thatcher."

"That's right." Pop smiled after giving Micah a quick pat on the shoulder. "See you this afternoon, squirt."

"Bye, Pop." He smiled, then let Dad take him into the classroom with a bunch of other boys and girls.

"Our turn, baby girl." Pop led her a few doors down. "Is this the right one?" he asked, stopping to look at the name block.

She looked at the note in her hand. "Mrs. Fells." She nodded.

Pop let her take him inside. Chelsea's eyes were trying to take in everything. The colors, the letters, the pictures. There was so much! "They have books!" She tugged on his hand in their direction.

"Why don't we see what we're supposed to do first. Remember the rule: Listen to the teacher."

She looked up at her Pop. "Listen to the teacher. I ask if I can look at the books, right?"

"Right. They might have a reading hour, or special time for the books. Everything will be explained."

"And who is this darling?"

Her Pop shook hands with the lady who'd spoken. "Parker Vandersoot. And this is Chelsea Vandersoot-Parkinson, but we shortened it for their sakes."

The other lady laughed kindly. "I don't doubt it!" She smiled for Chelsea. "I'm Mrs. Fells, your teacher this year. I can see you're excited to get started."

Chelsea hopped on her toes.

"Why don't you put your backpack under the table with your name on top. Once all the kids are here, we'll go over the rules of the room."

"Rules," she echoed.

"Just like at home, baby girl," Pop said gently.

They found her table and she slid her backpack under the chair. Pop crouched low to talk to her. "Okay, honey. I have to go so you can learn. You listen to Mrs. Fells. You're going to have a fun day and when you and Micah get home, I want to hear about all of it."

"You'll be there? After school?" She bit her lip, only a small twitch of fear pinching her.

"After school, and every day," he replied solemnly.

She leaned close, relieved. "Love you, Pop."

He did the same, whispering, "Love you back." He kissed her cheek lightly then stood straight. "See you at two twenty." She watched him walk out the door and thought she heard him talking to Dad, too. Mrs. Fells was getting other kids to their seats, so she had to be patient.

She pulled out her chair and sat, waiting like Pop had explained.

"Hi," a girl said at her side.

Chelsea turned and smiled. "Hi."

"I'm Miranda."

"Chelsea."

Miranda smiled. "Want to play at recess?"

Chelsea nodded hard. She couldn't wait!

About the Author

Diana DeRicci is the sexy, flirty pen name of Diana Castilleja. A romance author at heart, DeRicci's writing takes you into a saucier spectrum of sensuality and sexual adventure, where a happily-ever-after is still the key to any story. Diana lives in Central Texas with her husband, one son, and a feisty little Chihuahua named Rascal. You can catch the latest news on all of Diana DeRicci's writing and books on her website. Feel free to drop Diana an email. She'd love to hear from you.

Visit her on the web at:
www.DianaDeRicci.com

PURPLE SWORD PUBLICATIONS
www.purplesword.com